Back Cover

Historical Romance

THE EARL OF CADE HAD given up the battle of his emotions. Travis had fought as hard as he was able, and lost. He knew beyond doubt that Elizabeth would always be lodged in his heart. He'd made the decision to keep her near him, but vowed she would never have the least inkling of how strongly he desired her.

Never knowing when another painful health crisis would strike again, he reinforced the knowledge he could never marry.

But Elizabeth has her eyes set on him. Will he be able to resist her charms?

1

MuseItUp Publishing
https://museituppublishing.com
Cover Art © 2017 by Charlotte Volnek
Layout and Book Production by Lea Schizas
eBook ISBN: 9781771279499
Print ISBN: 9781393438878
First eBook Edition *October 2017

To my wonderful family, each and every one.

My Elusive Earl

Jean Hart Stewart

MuseItUp Publishing
www.museituppublishing.com

Chapter One

ELIZABETH SNORTED. A most unladylike snort, but one she'd dearly love to make even louder. Fuming, she wished she knew enough gutter words to express her disgust with this brute of a man. A beefy man now pushing his horse against her own and forcing her into a bramble bush besidethe path.

Tossing her head in disgust, her thick braid tangled in the thorns of the bush. Trying to pull the tawny strands loose, she almost screamed with frustration when her long hair remained securely caught. That's what she got for riding around being comfortable instead of respectably putting up her hair.

"Leave me, Squire." Her haughty tones showed no sign of the panic she felt. "I'll never in this world marry you. Nor will I *ever* sell you Kimberly. Go. I no longer wish to speak to you."

The Squire sneered, his delight evident at finding his quarry pinned helplessly. He paid no attention to her demand to back away. Instead, he pressed his horse forward ruthlessly, backing her even further into the brambles.

She gasped, but then stopped trying to free her hair when a deep masculine voice unexpectedly spoke in a voice of authority.

"You will remove yourself, sirrah, or I will do it for you. Back your horse from the lady's. Immediately!"

The Squire seemed not to hear the new voice and tried to press forward, obviously delighted to have his quarry pinned.

Elizabeth looked up to see an impressive gentleman on an equally imposing black stallion. The man appeared to be quite tall, even seated with military erectness in his saddle. He was sparely but powerfully built, and his lean face with its prominent cheekbones and deep-set eyes personified authority and confidence. Dark hair curled slightly over his collar. Although a trifle thin, the thighs gripping the horse were corded with sinewy muscle.

He wheeled and rode directly up to the Squire, using the power of his magnificent stallion to force the other man's horse away from the girl's. She breathed a small sigh, and finished loosening her hair from the brambles. The bully exploded, brandishing his whip.

"Here, who the bloody hell do you think you are? Get your brute away from me."

"I'm Travis Rivington," the new arrival said coldly. He scorned to take notice of the whip, and fixed the man with a steely stare.

"Means nothing to me, you clodpole," blustered the Squire. "Get out of here and leave us alone. You have no right intruding in a friendly conversation between neighbors."

The newcomer turned to the girl.

"Was it a friendly conversation, Miss Drayton?"

Elizabeth's eyes widened. How did he know her name? Surely she couldn't have forgotten meeting such an impressive male!

"It was in no way a friendly conversation, sir. How could it be when Squire Bellamy is telling me if I do not marry him willingly he will force me to do so? Do you call that even amiable?"

Travis watched as her magnificent grey eyes, framed with sooty black lashes, flashed with fire.

The Squire turned almost purple. "Elizabeth, how dare you repeat our private conversation in front of a stranger? This is no concern of his!"

Travis Rivington spoke in a tone that would have caused his acquaintances in London to run for shelter.

"Anything that concerns Miss Drayton concerns me. I am the Earl of Cade."

"Good lord," gasped Elizabeth.

Turning toward her, his face softened momentarily into a smile.

"I try to be, I really do, but it's sometimes difficult."

His heart gave an odd little lurch as she looked at him in consternation, her eyes startled, with a different kind of anger now showing in their depths.

Looking at her made Travis feel slightly out of balance. He had not expected her to be so lovely. He drew a very deep breath. His exhaustion must account for the intensity of his unwanted reaction. Travis knew well he could have no lasting interest in any woman.

He confronted the Squire again, his voice soft, but ringing with indomitable resolution.

"I am Miss Drayton's legal guardian. If you wish to speak of marriage, it will first be with me. I will consider an appointment if you request it."

His tone left little doubt such a request would not be kindly received. Unbelievably, the Squire grew even more livid.

"If you are the Earl of Cade, which I doubt," he sneered, "you are known to have neglected Elizabeth for months. She won't listen to a thing you say. The whole village detests you."

Travis shrugged, but did not drop his daunting stare.

"That is between Miss Drayton and me. You can be assured I am indeed the Earl of Cade, that I take my responsibilities seriously, and that Miss Drayton alone is entitled to any explanation. I suggest you leave now."

His stance, even seated on his horse, was that of a warrior ready for combat. Bellamy muttered under his breath, and spurring his horse viciously, rode away. He cast a glance back at them both that promised retribution.

TRAVIS DIDN'T RELAX his posture, even though he was beginning to wonder how long he could stay in the saddle. The ride from London had been grueling, and a host of fiends seemed to be attacking his leg. Still, he was months late in seeking out his ward, and he wanted to have this over and done with. He forced himself to speak lightly.

"What an unpleasant individual! I trust you do not have many such in these parts."

He cautiously eyed Elizabeth, who had frozen into near rigidity. The girl grateful for rescue was gone. In her stead was an icy young lady.

"My lord Cade," she said scornfully, "I suppose good manners oblige me to thank you for your assistance just now. I cannot, however, call your appearance timely."

Travis sighed inwardly. He had feared she'd be difficult, but then she had a right to be. Even if he kept his seat on the horse, he wasn't sure he could walk when he dismounted. Still, he'd better not let that anger fester.

He answered her calmly. "Miss Drayton, we have much to discuss. I would ask only that you acquit me of being a villain until you hear me out. May I follow you back to Kimberly?"

"I can hardly refuse, my lord."

He thought a snowstorm could not be colder than her manner.

She absently patted her mare, who snickered and lifted her pretty head. Travis wondered if he should mention that the housekeeper at Kimberly had told him Miss Drayton was out riding on a bay mare with a white blaze on its nose, and that she was the prettiest young lady in the county. She was much more than that, he thought. At least he was going to be able to offer his explanations, even though it would probably be wiser to go to the inn where his man awaited him. No, surely his strength would hold out for a while longer, and the ever-present pain in his leg was something he had long endured.

He forced himself to sit even straighter and followed her.

When they reached the graveled drive to Kimberly, Elizabeth vaulted out of her saddle. After handing the reins to an old stableman, she stalked into the house.

Travis sat still, thankful for the moment's respite. He did not relish her seeing his awkward dismount. With a small unconscious sigh, his strong fingers briefly massaged the muscles in one hip. He could ignore the pain, but wanted to avoid a cramp that might cause a disastrous stumble. The stableman waited silently until Travis dismounted, and then asked if his lordship would like that huge horse cooled and fed. Travis sighed with relief when Palisades went readily with the man. At least Palisades was tractable, even if just for the present.

As he entered the hallway, Elizabeth turned impatiently and, for the first time, noted his limp. Her eyes widened only slightly, but her voice was subdued as she asked if he would care to follow her into the parlor. She called for tea, and then settled gracefully onto a faded and stiff-looking settee. She motioned Travis to the one comfortable looking chair in the shabby room.

ELIZABETH GAVE A HALF-smile. She was glad he was not a creditor. She would hate to owe money she didn't have to someone who could so competently face down the Squire! Then her feelings of resentment resurfaced as she turned to him.

She waited until Melinda had brought the tea, complete with fresh scones. Elizabeth looked at her questioningly, but the housekeeper did not explain the unexpected treat.

Neither said a word, until the scones had disappeared. Despite her disapproval of him, she couldn't help but be gratified to see him enjoying the food.

Travis looked up at her with a grin.

"You have obviously decided to be merciful and let me explain at my own pace. I appreciate your courtesy."

She gave him a cursory nod, and waited, stiffening in automatic rejection of any explanation he might make.

He spoke almost formally, the grin changing to a slight but appealing smile.

"I know well you deserve an explanation, Miss Drayton. You wrote the then Earl of Cade six months ago when your father died, asking for his advice as your legal guardian. His lawyer wrote to you of the Earl's own demise and that his brother was succeeding to the title and would be in touch. Since then you have heard nothing."

Elizabeth gave a stiff nod of assent, and looked startled as a new thought chased itself across her expressive face.

"But you can't be the brother. You are far too young!"

Travis hoped she didn't realize how much he enjoyed watching her. She was disarmingly easy to read. Those clear grey eyes were incapable of deceit.

"You are correct, Miss Drayton, and that was the problem. The brother was no sooner Earl than he was killed in a carriage accident. Events were thrown into confusion by the two unexpected deaths. After several months, the lawyers finally tracked me down and found me in a hospital in Portugal. As a distant cousin to the new Earl, I had never once thought to inherit."

Her openness enchanted him. Now it was clear she was torn between wondering if she'd made a mistake, and feelings of concern he'd been in a hospital. That was a period of his life he did not intend to discuss. He wanted no man's, or woman's, pity.

"It was some time before I could return to England and take up my new duties. By then, affairs were disastrously unorganized. I only found out last week that you and your brother are my welcome charges. I came at once to see how you were faring."

She looked so stricken that he added quickly, "I'm more than sorry it took so long. I can only tell you the confusion was great. I hope you and I can start with a fresh understanding and I'll do my best to redress the wrongs from the delay."

Elizabeth bent her head and stared at her hands. It was evident she felt guilty for her misjudgement of him, as well as the way she'd lashed out at him. He found her confusion delightful.

Travis's heart gave a quick thud as he looked down at her shining hair. A fawn color streaked with gold, the heavy braid was now charmingly disordered. She was a darling, her face not only beautiful but marked by intelligence, candor, and an underlying strength. He thought it a most unusual combination. He had not bedded a woman since before that last battle in Portugal, and his body was telling him he could easily overlook the fact he was her guardian.

He felt an almost irresistible urge to touch that flawless skin. Since he had no future with any woman, he'd do well to guard his actions, as well as his emotions.

He had nothing but sorrow to offer any woman.

"My lord," Elizabeth finally said, "I trust you will forgive my evil thoughts of you. I truly thought you were a villain."

"I hope I am not," Travis said gently. "As I told you, I am trying to be a good lord. There is much I have yet to learn. But for now, I'll be happy if you forgive my neglect."

Elizabeth looked up with a blazing smile. Travis quickly lowered his lashes. He did not want her to have any idea of how she affected him. She literally made his heart stutter.

"My lord, you can't know how relieved I am to shed my burden of contempt. Such feelings are very hard on the bearer, you know. I hope we can be friends."

He looked at her, pleased with her generous honesty.

"As do I. But may we take up our conversation tomorrow? My man Phillips is waiting for me at the Thistle Inn. If you will excuse me, I'll join him there and return in the morning.

His face was gray with fatigue, and Elizabeth noticed for the first time how it was marked with white lines of pain. She felt that in spite of his iron control, he was fast reaching the end of his strength. She must make this leave-taking short, and send him on his way.

Almost babbling, she started toward the door.

"You must meet Richard, of course, and my Aunt Lavinia, who came to us when Papa died. And you'll want to see the estate books, and as much of the farm as you wish. I hope to see you in the morning, then."

She opened the door and almost waved him through it.

Murmuring assent, Travis asked for Palisades to be brought to him, and made his awkward way to the horse.

As Elizabeth watched him, pity and concern chased across her mobile face. Two facts were glaringly clear. He obviously still suffered from his wounds. And he held her future in his hands. She not only was swept by compassion, but she wondered if he would have the strength, or even the inclination, to help her save Kimberly. He puzzled her. He was courteous and kind, but with a wall of reserve that seemed made of stone.

He was finally here, impressively here, but what would he do?

In truth, what could he do?

Chapter Two

TRAVIS HAD BEEN OVER-fatigued and in too much pain to get the sleep he badly needed. He'd spent much of the night slowly pacing the floor.

His muscles finally relaxed enough to let him fall into bed towards dawn and snatch some rest. The countenance he presented to Elizabeth in the morning was one of cheerful good humor. The pain was his alone. He never let it distress others.

Elizabeth opened the door herself, dressed in a morning gown of yellow and an equally bright smile.

She ushered him into the hall. As he followed haltingly along, he marked the signs of reduced circumstanced. Faded furnishings, marks on the wallpaper where pictures had once hung; the fact there appeared to be very few servants. The furniture was antique and of quality, but noticeably sparse.

"It is a beautiful morning, my lord. Have you had breakfast? Can we offer you something?"

"I broke my fast at the inn, Miss Drayton, but I thank you. I'd really like to get started on learning to know the estate. I feel woefully in arrears."

"Then won't you come in the parlor and tell me where you want to start? How can you even pick which of our problems is the most important?"

She spoke as if in jest, but he suspected she was more than half in earnest.

"Richard," he said simply. "I want to meet Richard. I don't imply he is a problem, but he is certainly important. As my wards you are both very important!"

He spoke with a smile, but she did not underestimate his sincerity.

"That at least is easy. I will fetch him," she said, and turned, excusing herself.

Returning shortly, she had a tow-headed boy by the hand. He looked at Travis with an interested, solemn expression, but no fear.

"Richard, make your compliments to Lord Cade. As you know, he is your guardian until you are twenty-one."

Richard was a very attractive ten-year-old, with his sister's gray eyes and open expression. Not awed by meeting his guardian, but obviously wary, he performed a satisfactory bow.

"My Lord Cade," he said. "You are most welcome."

Travis reached out and took the boy's hand, as he would have a man's. He did not want this boy against him as his sister had been.

"You and I have much to discover about each other, Richard. I have so many things to ask you. For instance, how do you like your tutor, and what are your favorite subjects? Do you like sports? But we will have plenty of time to explore these and other matters."

The words and the smile charmed Richard. Elizabeth had explained Lord Cade's delay, and he was cautiously prepared to at least tolerate his guardian. He had not, however, expected the Earl to shake hands with him, nor to be interested in his opinions.

"But Eliza is my tutor, sir, so of course I like her. She is a very good one. Although she makes me spend too much time on Greek and Latin."

Travis smiled at the common schoolboy complaint, and filed away the knowledge there was no money for a tutor and that Miss Drayton was well educated herself. Neither fact surprised him.

"We will discuss all this at length, Richard. As I say, we have years to get acquainted. I think now I want to ride around Kimberly with your sister."

"On that big, black horse? My lord, he is magnificent! Have you had him long?"

"He's been with me since he was a colt."

"Then you trained him yourself?"

Travis smiled indulgently. Everyone admired Palisades, and with reason. He was a magnificent horse, both in form and intellect.

"Indeed I did, Richard, and it is a good thing for me he's so intelligent. He saved my life several times during the war."

The moment Travis made that statement he regretted it, as Richard's eyes lit up. He had forgotten how little boys thought war was fascinating.

"How famous, sir! Would you tell me about it? Do you think I could ever ride him? I'd be very careful! I'm really an excellent rider."

Travis decided to let his lecture on the horrors of war go until another time. It was more important Richard understood Palisades was forbidden territory.

"As to riding him, I can't say 'no' emphatically enough, Richard, and I trust you will understand. Palisades has never let another being on his back. Never. To even attempt it would be extremely dangerous."

He spoke sternly, but in a kind tone.

Elizabeth sent a subdued Richard off to his studies, and suggested she and Lord Cade start their tour of the farm. As the horses were brought round, she introduced him to Jimson, the elderly stable master who had insisted on staying in her service. Jimson looked on with approval as Travis handed her up on her mare. Her eyes flew involuntarily to Travis'. His hand was firm and hard, an intriguing contrast to her own, and yet so very warm! It seemed to spread its heat through her body. She'd been handed up by other men, and felt nothing!

How strange!

They started across the farm. She hoped with all her heart Lord Cade would see Kimberly's promising future, instead of its dilapidated state. It had been a prosperous estate once, and could be again. Most of the tenants had been forced to leave when their houses became unlivable from lack of repair. Many were still in the village, and would be eager to come back if they had a place to live and farm.

She watched him anxiously as the day went by. His questions showed a depth of information about farming that surprised her.

TRAVIS WAS EQUALLY surprised by her knowledge. He volunteered little, however, and kept his thoughts to himself. It was hourly more apparent to him that a massive infusion of men and money was needed. He was amazed she'd been able to hold on this long. The disrepair was of long standing. Regardless of how excellent a father he'd been in other areas, his neglect of the estate meant to pass to his son had been nothing short of criminal. Travis despised anyone leaving his own children in such confusion. He'd have to be very careful of how he handled this. He certainly could not show his disgust for a man who'd doubtless been a beloved father.

He refused to answer Elizabeth's tentative probes for his reaction. Instead, he completely surprised her. At the end of the day, as they were riding slowly back to the house, he turned to smile at her.

"I am going to be completely unforgivable, Miss Drayton, after just managing to get somewhat back into your good graces. May my man Phillips and I impose on your hospitality? I'd like to come tomorrow, and stay here at your home until we get matters in hand. I not only need a great deal of information, but I distrust your Squire Bellamy. I would be here for that reason alone."

Elizabeth's instantaneous reaction was sheer elation. '*Now where did that come from?*' she wondered. This was a man whose very name she'd disliked. She'd known him for only one day! Granted, his physical presence was impressive, and he exuded a protective aura that was seductive. Doubtless this last was his attraction. She'd been alone with her worries for so long. His being lame was nothing compared to the air of strength he projected.

"My lord, of course we would be delighted! I would have suggested it myself, but feared our lack of the type of accommodations you're used to. We'll do our best to make you and your man comfortable, and certainly we can do as well as the Thistle Inn!"

Lord Cade did not look up, his hands full of a restive Palisades, who was far too interested in Firebird, Elizabeth's definitely flirty mare.

"Having guests will be such a treat for us all! Aunt Lavinia will be in alt."

Elizabeth fairly beamed at Travis, who showed his own pleasure with a smile.

"Then I'll send word to Phillips to bring our baggage and the landau today, if this pleases you. We can surely get much more accomplished if I am on the spot."

He did not add that omitting the long ride to and from the inn would benefit his physical strength. Surely an advantage, but he was more worried about Squire Bellamy. A bully who he judged would stoop to any tactics. He thought Elizabeth to be in some danger. Shaken at how the very thought of her in the Squire's hands undid him, he shook his head as if to clear it. An image of Elizabeth pinned beneath that brute's body had distracted him more than once during the long night. He wanted to be here if Bellamy appeared with any claims. He'd already written his man of business do some investigating of the Squire. Bullies often left a trail.

Damn it, he was becoming far too engrossed in his ward. It was dangerous for them both. Nothing could come of any close relationship. He knew full well he must not entice her, even inadvertently. Damned difficult, when he longed to undo that thick braid and run his hands through her gorgeous hair!

He tamped down his wicked thoughts on what else he'd like to do with his hands and that enticing body. He was her guardian, and nothing more.

He was a miserable cad. He shouldn't even have to remind himself this lovely girl could never be for him.

Chapter Three

THE HOUSEHOLD SETTLED into a routine that pleased them all. Phillips and Richard became bosom friends, with Phillips telling war tales to the lad as a reward for diligence in his studies for the day. Travis didn't suspect Phillips' stories were mostly about his master's bravery; he only knew the boy's study habits had become exemplary. Elizabeth was elated. She knew Richard loved her dearly, but he took advantage of her far too often, neglecting his studies to escape and run wild in the fields.

Aunt Lavinia was delighted someone might possibly help her two beloved charges. She'd grieved when Elizabeth had been forced to sell one treasure after another. Blue Fire and Firebird would have had to go soon, and she knew Elizabeth's deep love for the two thoroughbreds. She also knew the estate's hopes for the future were pinned on breeding them. So Lavinia watched and prayed.

Melinda was pleased to have two extra and appreciative men who devoured her excellent cooking. Jimson, like Lavinia, looked on and hoped.

Travis kept his counsel. Elizabeth had grown to know him as fair and knowledgeable, but not talkative. She was content, and trusted him. She would not try to force his confidence.

On the first night of his stay with them, Travis had spotted a chessboard in the parlor.

He cocked an eyebrow at Elizabeth.

"It looks well worn. I take it you play?"

She looked down, but not quickly enough to hide her little smile.

"I do, my lord, and fairly well. Would you like a game? I assure you it is far better than my singing or playing the pianoforte." She smiled at him sweetly.

So there had once been a pianoforte, he thought. "Yes, I would like a game. And I don't know why, but I think I might regret this. As a guest, I presume you will offer me the white?"

Elizabeth managed to look indignant.

"Certainly not, my lord. As a female who needs every advantage, I get to choose. Naturally I take the white."

She smiled so brilliantly he caught his breath, feeling his heart bounce. He hastily looked down and began placing the chessmen in their proper positions. His sternness gave him the look of a formidable opponent, but Elizabeth smiled more broadly, lowered her eyes and made her first move.

Travis looked up sharply. It was a move that could be made by either a rank amateur, or an experienced player. He now had little doubt which one she was.

The advantage moved back and forth as it became apparent they were almost equally skilled. Elizabeth at first found it hard to concentrate. She kept looking at his elegant hands, with their faint dusting of hairs across the back. His long fingers moved gracefully and almost seemed to caress the pieces. She loved to watch their movement as he would hesitate, and then slowly move to pick up exactly the right piece. She told herself to stop staring. She was up against a master player, and needed all her wits to be victorious. He scattered them all too easily.

As she increased her concentration, she bent her head over the board. She'd jerked off her ribbon and her lustrous hair flowed over her shoulders. Her lovely scent entranced Travis. It was too light to be roses, but it was definitely floral. Ah, he had it. Lilacs! The fragrance was like Elizabeth, Travis thought. Fresh and enchanting, and not usual at all.

He'd damned well better concentrate.

When Aunt Lavinia tried to swallow her yawns, Elizabeth took pity on her. Intrigued by facing such a challenging opponent, she felt exhilarated enough to go on for hours. But she noticed the fatigue and pain lines were again etched on Travis's drawn face.

She sat back in her chair and shrugged.

"You have me, my lord, in about six moves. I will concede you the game, and not gracefully. You are a truly excellent player."

"As are you, Miss Drayton. But I call your concession more than graceful since I am not convinced I would have won, and refuse to accept. Is Richard a good player also?"

"Very good. Papa would have none other in the house. You are most generous, so we'll have to play a rematch tomorrow night."

Murmuring his assent, and bidding both ladies goodnight, he moved awkwardly from the room. Elizabeth watched him go. He puzzled her. Certainly his protective aura was appealing. Why was it when with him, she sometimes forgot to breathe? She'd never before felt this way when talking to a man, and she was not sure she liked it. It seemed a decidedly odd reaction. More important, his innate reserve kept her from knowing what he truly felt about anything. That, she knew she didn't like at all.

On the fourth day, Elizabeth and Travis were closeted in the small office going over the accounts. They were deep in a discussion of whether hops should be planted in the lower pasture, when a frantic neighing erupted from the barn.

Travis was on his feet instantly.

The Earl threw down the pad of paper he'd been writing on and headed for the stables. He recognized this furious neighing as Palisades'. Travis went quickly, loping in a gait so awkward it made Elizabeth wince. She could only imagine how painful it was for him, when he had always moved his body so carefully. Elizabeth hurried after him, finally running, but she could scarcely keep up. It seemed to her that his every step became more lumbering. She noticed as she neared the stable that Jimson was also coming at a run from the far corner of the corral.

As they neared Palisades' stall, the neighing became more and more enraged. Flinging open the door, Travis immediately spotted Richard, cowering in a corner, holding a carrot in his trembling hand. Palisades' eyes were rolling in rage, his lethal hooves raised and about to slam down.

Chapter Four

AS ELIZABETH WATCHED in horror, the big, black horse reared and pounded the wall behind Richard with deadly force. Richard covered his head with his arms, and curled his body to make himself as small as possible. Palisades, half demented with fury, raised up to strike again, his huge body lending all its weight to the power of those iron-shod hooves. Travis shouted at him to get his attention, and moved directly in front of his horse. Palisades stopped rearing, but his eyes were still half-crazed as he pawed the ground frantically.

Travis spoke in a soft and deadly tone.

"Richard, I want you to slip out behind me. *Immediately.* I will talk to Palisades while you get out of the stall. Move slowly."

There was every possibility Palisades' fury would keep him from recognizing the voice of the owner he loved. While Elizabeth and Jimson held their breath, Travis advanced, talking softly to the big horse, eventually reaching up and stroking his nose. The tone was that of a lover, assuring Palisades of his wonderful prowess, how there had never been a horse so skilled, and how proud Travis was of him. He was almost crooning, desperately reaching for the mind of his frantic horse.

Elizabeth grabbed Richard to her as soon as he crept behind the Earl to safety. The terrible chance the Earl was taking horrified her, and while she held Richard tightly, she couldn't tear her gaze away from Travis and his horse. The big beast slowed his pawing, and finally stopped and stood shuddering. His massive chest heaved heavily, and although his eyes no longer looked demented, he was far from calm.

Travis stood, his hand stroking Palisades, his eyes never wavering from those of the horse. His voice was quiet and steady. He did not turn, but spoke calmly to Elizabeth and Richard, whom were now behind him.

"I want both of you to go back to the house. I will stay with Palisades until I am sure he is himself."

"My lord, began Richard tearfully, "I beg you—"

"Not now, Richard. Oblige me by doing as I have said."

It was the voice of the commanding officer. The tone was quiet, but the sternness left no doubt he was to be obeyed. Elizabeth had a momentary vision of Travis Rivington on the battlefield, deploying his troops in just such an implacable manner. She had no doubt his composure would have impressed even the most rebellious or frightened soldier. Elizabeth shivered, not understanding at all the thrill that ran through her, seeming to heat and chill her at the same time.

Disobedience was out of the question.

Richard, tears streaming down his face, turned and ran toward the house. Elizabeth ached to follow him, but instead, stood slightly to one side of the stable door. Something about the rigid control the Earl was displaying alarmed her. While one part of her urged her to comfort Richard, something else ordered her to stay where she was.

Jimson came to the opening of Palisades' stall, and slowly put one foot in and then stopped. After a few moments of tossing his head and whinnying, the huge horse allowed Jimson to approach him. Jimson began to also stroke and talk to the horse, and as Travis saw the danger was truly past, he turned and walked stiffly out of the stall.

Just outside he slumped abruptly to the ground. Elizabeth rushed to him, bending over him as he sat, his head on his knees, his tousled black hair all that she could see.

"Get Phillips," he muttered. The words were not clear, as if he could scarcely force them through his teeth.

Elizabeth immediately turned to rush toward the house. Just then Phillips appeared, running. Quite evidently he'd heard the big stallion's commotion and knew it to be dangerous. He hurried to his master and bent over him.

"Oh, milord, " he wailed, "not again! I had hoped you were over these spells."

"Get me to the house, man," Travis gritted out. "And get Miss Drayton out of here."

"Yes, sir, right away, milord. Can you walk at all?"

"I'm not sure. I'll try. After Miss Drayton leaves."

Elizabeth realized the Earl's pride made him detest her seeing him in such a humiliating condition. Accordingly she turned away and scurried to the house, calling out orders to prepare the Earl's bedchamber, and to send immediately for the doctor. This last posed something of a problem, for Jimson and Phillips were undoubtedly needed to help the Earl. She thought of dispatching Richard, but decided he was too overwrought, and more importantly, the stable boy could probably ride faster. She would go herself but for the knowledge Travis or Richard might need her. Accordingly, she detoured on the way to the house and dispatched William, with admonishments to go as fast as he could, and bring back the doctor immediately.

Staying well out of sight, she lingered to observe the Earl. She watched with horror as Jimson and Phillips knelt beside the Earl, and placed one of his arms around each of their necks. Slowly and carefully they lifted him to his feet and began the long walk to the house. She heard his involuntary groan, and was horrified to see he was almost helpless. He strove gallantly to put one foot in front of the other, but could not. After a few yards, she saw him go completely slack, and realized he had lost consciousness.

"Thank Gawd," said Phillips. "Let's hope we can get him in bed before he revives. He will feel less pain this way. Gently, man, gently. Let's get the Captain to the house."

Elizabeth began to run, calling to her aunt as she entered the house. She wanted his room ready when he was carried to it, and everyone out of the way while the men got him settled. She herself stayed just outside the door of his room after they carried him in, hearing only rustling sounds that meant outer clothing was being removed and the Earl was being placed in his bed.

It seemed a very long time before Dr. Stratford arrived. He shut the door behind him, and all she could hear was the rumble of voices, the Earl's deep tones now wavering and unsteady. The doctor, who had brought her and Richard into the world, as well as caring for her parents, finally appeared with a grave face.

He shut the door carefully behind him.

"That is a very injured man, Elizabeth, as well as a brave one. I can do little for him, although I insisted he take a dose of laudanum. I vow if he had not been so weak I would not have prevailed, as he's not the type to make it easy for himself. He will get some rest tonight. I cannot answer for tomorrow. I'll of course come to check him, although there is little I can do to help."

Elizabeth walked the doctor to the front door, and thanked him. She was completely shaken. What on earth could cause such a devastating collapse in such a controlled man? She returned to the bedroom and knocked softly on the door. Phillips opened it almost immediately, and at her pleading look, motioned her in. She moved to the bedside, where the Earl lay motionless. Deep pain lines were etched into his white face, and her heart turned over with pity.

"Never fear, ma'am. He is not unconscious. The laudanum the good doctor insisted on is giving him some rest. He will never take it from me, and I imagine he will refuse it tomorrow. He has a monstrous fear of becoming dependent on any drug. He saw too much of that in the hospital. Gawd knows he could use more help than he allows himself."

"I take it this has happened before," said Elizabeth, looking down at the sleeping Earl.

Despite the pain lines, his face in repose seemed younger and sweeter. She stood gazing at him, free to stare at his attractively strong features, and thinking how very handsome he was. She had an urgent wish to smooth his tousled hair from his face. Glancing at Phillips, she refrained.

"No, it is not rare, ma'am. I wish it was. Still, it's been some time since he's been taken as bad as this. For sure he's been overdoing, what with riding down from London, and then jaunting all over the farm. Running to the barn probably finished him off, although he wouldn't want Master Richard to think that."

"But what's wrong?" asked Elizabeth in a low, puzzled tone. "What gives him such terrible pain?"

"It's from the war, ma'am," Phillips said bitterly, but with a touch of pride in his Captain. "At Talavera, four of our men were pinned down by a sniper. The Captain crept around behind him and got him. He saved our men, Gawd bless him, but he took a bullet in his hip. I reckon the surgeon did the best he could, but the bullet had splintered and he couldn't get all the pieces out. Sometimes if he is too active, something shifts inside, and he suffers somethin' terrible. Sometimes he can't even move for a while. Gawd knows any one of his regiment would rather have taken the bullet. All his men worshipped him."

"And how long will it take him to get over it?" Elizabeth asked, pity and concern making her voice unsteady.

"No one can say, ma'am. The Captain lives in terror he won't never, and that in one of these spells he'll stay paralyzed. Unless I'm very wrong he'll force himself to move as soon as he wakes. The pain must be somethin' fierce when he does that."

"Do the attacks last long? How often do they come?"

"He can't tell when they are coming, nor how long they will last. Usually it's for three or four days. For my money I figure it lasts 'til the piece of bullet shifts again. Prob'bly him forcing himself to walk is the best thing he can do, although none of the damned doctors seem to have any idea how to help him. Beg your pardon for the language, ma'am, but it's a terrible thing for a young man like the Captain."

"But how does he stand such awful pain?" Elizabeth whispered.

"I don't know, ma'am. Gawd knows I don't think I could. He almost never takes the laudanum the docs want him to, but sometimes I can get him to drink brandy, and it helps. But that is only when he feels he's over the worst, and is moving again a little."

Her eyes widened with horror and a deep regret.

"Will you promise to call me if I can help in any way at all?"

At Phillip's word he would, she went off to find Richard. She found him in bed, exhausted and asleep after the emotional storm he had been through. Leaning over him, she kissed his forehead. She would try to temper his guilt and blame in the morning.

She lay awake a long time. As the Earl lay drugged and helpless from the laudanum, she had been able to stare at him as much as she wanted. She realized she was attracted by everything about him. He was irresistibly handsome, but his appeal was as much because of his character as his looks. She was captivated by his courtesy and his kindness. And his undeniable courage. She thought him the most admirable man she'd ever known. The sight of him produced an instant heat and quivering in her lower body that puzzled her. Reluctantly she recognized the fascination which had been present from almost the moment of their first meeting. She knew now how deeply he affected her. He made her whole body hum.

She must put a strong guard on her feelings. Not only was he an Earl, and very much above her, but he must not feel even more obligation than he did now. She'd be very careful not to let the attraction grow. Surely she could control it. She wondered briefly why she thought of Robbie Carstairs only as a beloved brother, even though he was just as handsome as the Earl. She did not feel at all sisterly toward Travis.

About four in the morning, she wakened suddenly. Usually the house at this time of night was completely silent, except for a few old-house mutterings. Those creaks she knew and ignored. This was completely different.

The sounds were coming from the Earl's bedroom, which was adjacent to hers. He was dragging himself around his room, pausing often, but never completely stopping. Remembering Phillips' words, she shuddered at the cost he was paying. Although she tried to go back to sleep, she could not, and simply lay there listening to the halting footsteps, suffering with the walker who strove not to be defeated.

Finally there was silence. Even the Earl's indomitable will must have decreed a stop. She closed her eyes, and slept fitfully, her cheeks damp with tears.

Chapter Five

ELIZABETH WALKED INTO the breakfast room the next morning, still consumed with worry about Travis. Phillips had sent no word. One look at the drawn faces of Aunt Lavinia and Richard and she knew she had to mask her own fears. Richard was obviously overwhelmed with guilt. Refusing to answer any questions about the Earl, she said only she would talk to him after breakfast.

None of them ate much and finally, pushing back her chair, she asked Richard to follow her. She certainly didn't want him to know the extent of the Earl's suffering. In his room she wrapped her arms around the boy and tried to reassure him he wasn't completely to blame for the Earl's collapse, but she could not in all honesty tell him he was blameless. She did stress the fact that the whole situation was something none of them could have foreseen.

"I wasn't trying to make trouble, Eliza," Richard gulped out. Tears welled in his eyes, and started spilling down his cheeks. "I only wanted to make friends with Palisades. He is *such* a horse, and I know I can never ride him. I just wanted to be his friend."

"We all know that, you clunch," said his sister, ruffling his hair. She wiped his face with her handkerchief and then handed it to him.

"Nobody is such a Bedlamite as to think you set deliberately out to make trouble. Unfortunately, Palisades was in the mood to be spooked, and a stranger in his stall set him off."

"Is the Earl really furious with me? He promised to talk to me about it, and hasn't. Does that mean he is so angry he will never forgive me? He's such a great gun, and I wouldn't cause him trouble for anything."

"I know, love. The Earl knows it. Please don't be so upset." Gathering him in her arms, something she had rarely done since he had grown older and more independent, she tried to soothe the distraught boy. Elizabeth murmured softly to him until the strain on his face eased a little.

"I'm going to try to see the Earl now," she told him. "He is very much a man of his word, and will talk to you as soon as possible. I'm sure he will not be angry with you. Please go to the schoolroom and work on your lessons. You know the Earl sets great store on learning. He would never break his word, and will soon talk to you. I'll go see how he is, and report back to you."

She found the door to the Earl's room again barred by Phillips.

"I'm sorry, Miss Elizabeth, but I can't let you in. The Earl told me to please make you his excuses, and he hopes to talk to you tomorrow."

Phillips very firmly shut the door. Elizabeth's shoulders sagged. There was nothing else she could do, except wait.

She'd never been much good at waiting.

During the next two days, Elizabeth applied herself even more strenuously than usual to the estate's affairs. She kept herself busy with every small task she could find. She checked on Palisades daily, and found the stallion restive and badly in need of exercise, but could do nothing except help Jimson lead him into the largest corral to run as best he could.

She slept fitfully, waking often to the sounds of the Earl's walking about his room. Phillips was most firm about letting no one in to see the Earl, and the whole household was unnaturally quiet as they went morosely about their routine.

On the fourth morning after his collapse, Elizabeth looked up from working on the books to find Phillips standing in the doorway.

"The Captain would like to see you now, miss, if you can spare the time. I was told to be particular to make sure it be convenient."

"Of course it is, Phillips, I will come at once."

She spoke sedately, but it was all she could do to keep from jumping up and running after Phillips. Nothing had ever been more important than finally seeing the Earl. Her heart beat erratically, and she hurriedly smoothed her hair and skirts.

Swishing excitedly into the room, she saw him seated in a chair by the window. She tried to mask her shock at his appearance, but his wry smile revealed he was well aware of her reaction. His eyes were deep sockets in his head, and he looked ten years older than when he had first arrived at Kimberly.

His black hair needed a barber, but she rather liked it long and curling slightly over his collar.

Despite his appearance, Travis' smile was welcoming, and she thought, genuinely sweet. His habitual air of aristocratic distance seemed for this moment, at least, suspended.

She advanced swiftly toward him, her hands outstretched, and he reached up and grabbed them with a strength that belied his appearance.

"My lord," she breathed softly, "it is so nice to see you up and smiling. How goes it with you?"

"My lady ward," he said, "I do well enough. And how does Richard?"

She was touched to her depths that after the terrible last days, his first words would be of her brother.

"Richard will do well enough now that you are better. I've tried to disabuse him of the notion that he alone caused your disturbance, but he feels dreadfully guilty. And in truth I think he has much to answer for. When you're up and about Richard will be well too. As it is, I think both of you are a little more pinched than I care to see."

A fleeting look of amusement chased across his features.

"Thank you for naming it only a 'disturbance'. I am sure it was much more than that to the entire household, and I truly beg everyone's pardon. As for Richard, I will see him later today. He does not have an ounce of meanness nor scheming in his body, and I'll reassure him as best I can. In the meantime, being bedridden, or near to it, gives one a great deal of time to think. I've come to some conclusions I wish to share with you, Elizabeth."

She realized he was using her name naturally, and as if he'd always done so. Perhaps he'd been calling her that in his thoughts for some time, as she had long thought of him as Travis. She certainly hoped so.

His distant sternness was nowhere in evidence. While still serious, he somehow seemed more accessible. Some wall between them had fallen. She felt as if she were dealing with an old and trusted friend. Not at all sure that this was the relationship she wanted, still, she thought it had possibilities. She waited for the decisions he had mentioned.

"First of all, let me assure you that I am quite taken with Richard. He is intelligent, and of a charming frankness. I would be happy if I could someday have a son exactly like him. Moreover, you have done an exemplary job of raising and teaching him. So I hope you will not condemn me when I tell you I've made the decision he is to be sent away to school."

Elizabeth blanched and tightened her hands into white fists. Her mind fairly screamed, 'No, no, not so soon!' She was well aware Richard needed more than she could give him. But there was no money for such a venture, nor could she imagine her daily life without him.

"I don't see how that is possible, my lord," she said stiffly.

"And why not, Elizabeth? Surely you know he needs stimulation and companionship, friends of his own age, and studies and sports to challenge him. He will go as my ward, and under my sponsorship."

Her chin went up.

"I suppose that means you intend to pay the shot, my lord," she said angrily. "You know I cannot permit such a thing. Overseeing our affairs and giving us advice is one thing, and your right, but I cannot consider allowing you to take on such a vast expense."

Travis steepled his hands and looked at her. There was a good deal of compassion and understanding in his glance, and an affection that at the moment she didn't want to see.

"Would you prefer me to bring the matter to the attention of your grandfather?"

Her head shot up. "My lord, our grandfather has never even met us! After my father married the woman of his own choice, but not my grandfather's, he completely cut his son off. I will not go to him now. He made no response when I sent word of my father's death."

"But Richard must be educated."

He watched as she battled tears, but said nothing. He longed to go to her and fold her in his arms, letting her know that he counted helping her as a distinct pleasure. He definitely could not hold her the way he desired, but hoped to deal gently with her pride.

"My dear," he continued, "I was very much afraid you would react in just this manner. But stop and consider. I must return to London. I cannot leave you both here. I tell you now that I not only mean to send Richard to school, but I am taking you to London with me."

Elizabeth blanched with shock.

"My lord! I have no wish to be at cuffs with you! But a more unreasonable set of suggestions, I have yet to hear! What of the farm? What of Aunt Lavinia? I must salvage the estate for Richard, and I cannot do it from London. And what would I do in London? I have no social polish, few of the social skills that are needed, and I certainly do not have the wardrobe! I would be as out of place as, as, an *ostrich* in London!"

In spite of his exhaustion Travis laughed. Leaning his head back against the chair he said softly, "I would never liken you to an ostrich, Elizabeth. That's not at all what you bring to my mind."

There was a warmth in his gaze that made Elizabeth feel cherished and cared for. Drat the man and his ability to discompose her. It would be so easy to sink into the seductive spell of his concern, and let him make all her choices. Even though he was still ill, his masculine strength and authority were amazingly evident. But she'd made all the decisions for her small household for too long to surrender easily.

Travis watched her, his eyes hooded. As usual, her emotions played across her expressive face, and as usual, he delighted in watching her. He sat silently, as he certainly didn't want her to realize the depth of his sympathy.

"I will talk to you soon, Elizabeth, about this *unreasonable set of suggestions*. But for now I beg your leave to continue this conversation at a later time. Try to consider calmly what I propose. I will definitely, however, talk to Richard this day. I find I need more periods of rest than I'd like. If you choose to tell him of my decision please do so, but be assured I'll not let the subject drop. I think you might be surprised at his reaction."

Elizabeth knew she couldn't press her arguments with a man recovering from a horrendous ordeal. She sat silently, struggling with her feelings.

"Elizabeth," he added softly, "I beg you acquit me of evil intentions. I will do nothing, nor allow anything to be done by others, that will harm you or Richard."

His gaze was direct and unwavering, and ordinarily she would have been reassured. But all her mind reiterated was he was sending both her and Richard away from their beloved home, and from each other? Nodding stiffly, she stalked from the room, her temper beginning to flare. She was determined to find Richard and tell him how obnoxiously his new hero was behaving. Imagine planning to separate them! And then she would tell Aunt Lavinia! They were both obviously mistaken in thinking the Earl was an exemplary character. They had one and all been deceived.

Chapter Six

SHE ABRUPTLY STOPPED her mad rush from the house. Could she count on the support of Aunt Lavinia? *Not at all!* Aunt Lavinia, in her anxiety to further her ideas of well-being for her two charges, was likely to be in favor of the whole preposterous plan. She'd think more schooling for Richard and social opportunities for Elizabeth to be just the thing! No, she couldn't count on Aunt Lavinia. She'd better find Richard at once.

She found him in one of his favorite haunts, the stream at the foot of the sheep pasture, digging up some of the ancient rocks that so interested him, a small but happy smile on his intent face. The day was golden and sunny, and Richard's bright curls shone like a beacon as she crossed the meadow. In a field nearby, a lark trilled his song of love to his ladybird. Wild daisies, small but exuberant, dotted the grass. Elizabeth suddenly had to clutch onto her composure as she thought of being forced to leave this beloved place. With an effort, she managed to address Richard calmly.

"Richard, I have good news for you. I have just been talking with the Earl, and he says he wishes to speak with you later today."

To her surprise Richard looked at her with clouded eyes, his previously sunny countenance overcast. Evidently his worries ran too deep to be dismissed by the mere knowledge the Earl was again conversing with the household.

"Does he really want to see me, Eliza? You can tell me the truth. Why has he kept to his room all this time? Was rescuing me from Palisades what injured him? You know I never meant any wrong."

His voice quavered and betrayed his agitation, as did the eyes suddenly damp with unshed tears.

Elizabeth mentally drew up short. She was on dangerous ground, fearing upsetting Richard any more deeply than he already was. If she criticized the Earl's plan of going away to school, it would sound like criticism of the Earl. She didn't think Richard could handle what he might perceive as an attack on his hero. She abandoned any idea of disclosing the Earl's intentions. Richard must never think it was his fault they were being sent away. The Earl would have to deal with that.

"No, no, love. Don't fret so. His illness is of long standing, and dates back to the war, as Phillips has told us. He is very fond of you, and looking forward to seeing you."

Richard still looked very unsure, but he did put down his rock and walked, half-skipping, back to the house with her.

"Then I had better get rid of some of my dirt, so I'm ready when he sends for me. You'll be sure to let me know as soon as possible, won't you, Eliza?"

Elizabeth chatted with him about how they must find more books to expand his interest in geology, and how pleased the Earl must be to hear he'd been working hard at his studies. Let Travis be completely responsible for telling Richard of his plans. She would not be accountable for making her brother feel any worse.

As they were just finishing lunch, Phillips appeared in the doorway.

"The Captain's been resting, ma'am, and would appreciate it if you and Master Richard could join him in his room. He's anxious to talk to you both that I don't think I can get him to settle down until he sees you."

His manner, although respectful, somehow told them he would prefer to keep everyone out of the Earl's room for the rest of the week.

Elizabeth and Richard exchanged concerned glances, put aside their pudding and followed Phillips to the Earl's bedroom. Travis sat in his armchair, resting his head against the back. He did not seem relaxed, as much as calmly determined.

"I thank you both for appearing so promptly. Richard, do come here and let me shake your hand. I know from Phillips that you have been most diligent about your studies since I last saw you. I'm truly sorry it took me so long to have my promised talk with you, and I beg your forgiveness."

Both Draytons were overcome by this gracious speech. Richard's eyes teared up as he walked over and grabbed the Earl's hand, holding it in both of his.

"But, sir, my lord, it is I who must beg forgiveness. I never meant to cause trouble by taking Palisades a carrot, but I know now it was a thoughtless thing to do. I do hope I have your pardon."

Travis smiled, that genuine smile that transformed his disciplined countenance, and ruffled the boy's hair.

"Then let us agree to forgive one another, and forget the matter. I have very important concerns to discuss with you and your sister, and would have your mind clear."

Even Elizabeth was amused at how Richard straightened his back and looked solemnly back at the Earl.

"To come to the point, Richard, I've concluded it's time to send you to school, the same one I attended at your age. You'll have to study very hard, but I know you are capable. And there'll many other boys there, some of whom are bound to become your good friends. In fact, if it's the same as when I went to school, a few will be friends for the rest of your life. Does that appeal to you?"

To Elizabeth's absolute astonishment, Richard's face lit as if illuminated by a host of candles.

"Oh, sir, how famous! Will there really be lots of boys? Will they want to be friends with me? I would so like to have friends. I have never really had one."

'But I'm your friend,' thought Elizabeth. 'I'm your best friend!'

Travis cast a swift and sympathetic glance at Elizabeth, and answered. "I can assure you there will be a great many boys. You will not like all of them, nor will all of them like you, but you are bound to form fast friendships with some. It is one of the chief advantages of public schooling."

A shadow suddenly darkened Richard's transparently glowing face.

"Eliza," he said, "What about Eliza?"

Turning anxious eyes toward her he asked, "Can you do without me, Liza? Maybe I should stay here with you. You do so much hard work now, I would not make it harder."

Before Elizabeth could clear her throat of the unexpected obstruction brought on by his sweetness, the Earl answered for her.

"But you have not heard all of my plans, Richard. Elizabeth will go with me to London. I have a sister, Claire, who is seventeen years old, very shy, and worried about making her come-out. I also have a mother who is hesitant about the turmoil involved in planning a come-out for a reluctant young lady. Your sister and Aunt Lavinia will be invaluable to them and to me in London. Surely you can see how grateful I'll be to them if they help us out."

Stunned into silence, Elizabeth yet had the wits to admire his masterful management. Richard was putty in his hands, and he had in one stroke cut the ground from under her feet. She had only one card left to play.

"If you had only mentioned some of these concerns sooner, my lord, we could have discussed them. It seems Richard is pleased to go to school, and Aunt Lavinia will be delighted with the idea of being in London and helping your lady mother. I shall miss them both, but naturally I can't abandon the farm. But I will cope."

Travis looked amused at her last attempt to squirm free of his machinations.

"Elizabeth, I've asked you before to acquit me of any villainy toward you and yours. I've written to Jack Crawley, a friend and fellow officer in my regiment, and invited him to be steward of Kimberly. He's a very good man, and has had difficulty finding work since he lost his left forearm in the war. I think you'll find him the most industrious steward you can imagine, and a man you will grow to like. But if you completely dislike him, of course we will search for another."

He looked at her with his usual direct gaze. He knew she was inwardly fuming. He longed to hold her and soothe her, but did not betray himself by even a gesture. His slight smile probably told her that he knew he had spiked all her guns and rolled her up. She would have a hard time refusing to give a chance to a wounded veteran.

So many men had gone to fight Napoleon, and had been hailed as heroes. Returning home, a great number seemed to find no place in the country they'd been defending. Veterans and their families were sleeping under hedgerows, and begging for food. Any person of feeling thought it a national disgrace, and Elizabeth was nothing if not empathetic. Still she would not abjectly capitulate.

She spoke defiantly, her eyes looking directly into his.

"Very well, my lord, you have outgunned me. However, if this Jack Crawley is as good as you say, he should be able to turn a profit here at Kimberly. I want an agreement you'll keep track of all expenses, for I'm well aware this will cost you a great deal. I want a strict accounting, for I insist on eventually repaying you."

She smiled a strained smile that dared him to say her nay.

Her head was high and her face flushed, and she looked adorably belligerent. Vastly relieved that the worst of the argument was behind him, the Earl agreed, although he had mental reservations about what he would tally as an expense and what would be his welcome duty to his wards. He would let that go for now, as there was still Aunt Lavinia to persuade. He felt she would be on his side, but could not be certain. She was the last obstacle in his determined path.

He would see that Elizabeth had her chance as well as Richard. Her chance to marry, and marry as she deserved.

Chapter Seven

TRAVIS HAD GIVEN UP the battle of his emotions. He had fought hard, but lost. He knew beyond doubt that Elizabeth would always be lodged in his heart. He'd made the decision to keep her near him, but vowed she would never have the least inkling of how strongly he desired her. She'd only to walk into the room and he wanted to tumble her to the floor. He'd not known he was even capable of the burning desire that he felt for her. If he were well, he would demand her hand in marriage and exert all his authority to see that she complied. But this last painful crisis had reinforced the knowledge that he could never marry, afraid for a while that he would never walk again.

He thought he could discipline himself to be with her and enjoy her, remembering that it was a God-given gift to be allowed to protect her. He would no longer be cold and distant. He could stop fighting his deep feeling for her and be her good friend. He would eventually guide her to an advantageous marriage.

There was no hurry about that, however. She'd have a season in London and learn the pleasures of town life. She'd be dressed properly to accent her unusual coloring and beauty, and she would meet his family. He would relish every bittersweet moment, reveling in her companionship, never forgetting that ultimately he must hand her over to another. But he would be damned sure that other was bloody well worthy of her!

To his amusement, Aunt Lavinia was as enthusiastic as he'd expected. Richard was counting the days, and the whole household awaited the arrival of Jack Crawley.

Travis' and Elizabeth's nightly chess game was still absorbing to both of them. They were almost evenly split on wins, even though Travis was an expert at forcing a draw when his men were in danger.

"Have you thought of the pluses of being in London at all, Elizabeth?" he asked her one night as she pondered a strategic move.

"Not really, my lord. I see few 'pluses', as you name them. I have no social skills. I find social talk meaningless. I don't know how to carry on with useless chatter. I fear your friends won't want to converse with a female who knows Mr. Thomas Coke's latest theory on crop rotation, but little else."

She spoke lightly, but he heard the underlying anxiety.

"I think you will find not all my friends are society fribbles," he answered. "And you'll certainly love the bookshops. You can find any book you have a yearning for, and many books you didn't even know existed."

He reveled in the light that sprang into her eyes.

"That is a most telling argument, you conniving man. I've long ago read everything in my father's library. Of course London will have everything! Books will be a joy indeed, but I don't imagine I can purchase very many. Just seeing the book stores will be enough!"

"Elizabeth, I have standing accounts at the stores, and anything you want I am sure will please my sister also. You will certainly be able to expand your reading."

She looked so defiant at the thought of spending his money that he winced. He should know better by now than to prick her pride.

"You will at least enjoy my library," he added softly. "You'll find many books there you will want to read. My mother and sister buy all the latest novels, and I've noticed there are mostly classics in your father's library."

Elizabeth's face was again illuminated.

"Do you have Lord Byron's works? I have not read any of them. I fear it a taste you might not approve, but I would dearly love to read some of the novels of Mrs. Radcliffe."

Travis laughed. "My sister has everything Mrs. Radcliffe has written, even though I think them rather gothically sensational. You might also enjoy Sir Walter Scott. If you like, we will visit Hatchard's bookshop on Piccadilly. It takes hours to begin to even notice what all they have."

The glow on her face told him he had picked the perfect topic to intrigue her.

"And the news will be much fresher," she said. "I sometimes long for the latest news and good conversation. I imagine that's an unfashionable sentiment for a young lady."

He smiled at her as he moved his hands into position to take her rook.

Elizabeth, again mesmerized by the long elegance of his fingers, sat waiting for his move. She thought of how she could discuss any topic with him, and not be afraid of his censure. Perhaps staying with him in London would not be so dreadful. No man had ever been so respectful of her opinions, and so little set on pushing his own. Since his illness she'd noticed his wall of reserve had lowered a little, allowing her to feel they were again good friends. It bothered her that she knew they wouldn't have as much time together in London. She'd quite come to count on his challenging companionship. Surely they had many days together before they left. She would enjoy every moment of them.

About a week later, Elizabeth looked up from the stable yard and saw a stranger riding toward the house. He was on a horse that was serviceable, but not handsome. His clothes were well worn, and meticulously brushed and clean. The sleeve of his jacket was pinned about half way up his left arm. It was obviously Jack Crawley.

She walked slowly up to the house.

She had such mixed feelings about so many things. She found Mr. Crawley being ushered into the parlor, where the Earl awaited him.

Travis rose and stretched one hand to the man as she stood looking on from the doorway.

"Jack, my friend. How good of you to come so quickly to help us out!"

Crawley grabbed his hand in obvious emotion.

"It is you, sir, who are good to me," he said. "Be assured I will do anything in my power to assist you."

Travis saw her approach and immediately introduced Crawley to her. He included her fully in the conversation as it turned to why Crawley had been sent for, and what the Earl wanted him to do.

She kept her peace, content to listen to the two men discuss the state of the farm. Suddenly Travis surprised her.

"Miss Drayton has drawn up an excellent long-range plan for needed repairs and improvements. Ah, I see by your raised eyebrows, Elizabeth, that you did not realize I had studied it. You gave it to me when I first arrived, along with the books. Had you forgotten, my dear?"

"I had not thought you paid it much mind, my lord," she answered with a dazzling smile. "I am flattered."

"I've not only studied it, I agree with it in every particular. It's well thought out, and I want Jack to start implementing it as soon as possible."

She thought it one of the nicest compliments she had ever received. Her face bloomed, and then clouded over as she remembered her first priority on the list.

"But, my lord, I listed repair to the tenant houses as the main concern. There is simply no money to countenance such a thing."

"We both know it's essential for an increase in men and capital to make Kimberly a paying venture. I see no reason this can't be done, and there must be some investment made. We have agreed, have we not, that you will repay me in the future?"

He looked on, hoping he was masking his sympathy. He understood her struggle. The estate was her only means of support, and she hoped to restore it so that someday Richard would have a worthy inheritance. Yet every proud fiber in her body resented taking money from another.

"Elizabeth, I promise I will keep accounts. You will pay me back when Kimberly is the property that it once was."

She turned anguished eyes on him and then left the room. She should be grateful to him for giving Kimberly a chance. He was, after all, doing exactly what she'd hoped. But accepting financial help was harder than she'd expected. She didn't think, moreover, that he was giving her a choice.

She found Phillips in the stable, talking to Palisades. The big horse tolerated a few people beside the Earl, even though he would not permit them to ride him.

Phillips brushed down Palisades as he chatted.

"So, my black beauty, do you remember our days on the Peninsula? This is a far different place, and better for us both, I'm thinking. I jes' wish the master could get over these awful spells of his."

Elizabeth walked in and patted Palisade's neck.

"You are indeed a beauty," she crooned. "And you know the Earl better than any of us. You can count yourself privileged, my big friend."

"Aye," said Phillips, "the three of us have been together a long time. Ever since the beginning, when Wellington wanted Portugal mapped so he could plan his campaign. The captain and I spent months scouting, and Wellington himself told us how he hated to let the Captain go."

"I did not realize that," Elizabeth said. "I knew you had been his batman, but I didn't know the relationship went back that far. No wonder you think so highly of each other."

Phillips drew himself up proudly.

"Major Rivington was the best officer in the army. When he got injured so badly, I had to stick with him to make sure he got treated right. Sometimes even the best men got little care in the field hospitals."

Elizabeth shuddered at the image his words conjured. Travis, injured and at the mercy of overworked hospital personnel. Thank God for Phillips.

She went on to the stable to caress Firebird. Jimson was exercising Blue Fire. She could see them in the distance. Blue Fire's mane streaming in the wind he was creating by his fast pace. Her beloved horses would be safe with Jack Crawley. She had no doubts of his dedication and ability.

She was almost back at the house when she saw Squire Bellamy's carriage come through the big gates, and hurtle up the cobblestone driveway. Going around to the back door, she arrived in the hall in time to hear him demand to see Miss Drayton. She could hear the muted voices of Travis and Crawley, and was relieved. She could not imagine a visit from the Squire being anything but disagreeable, and she blessed the fact the Earl was on hand.

"Miss Drayton is out, sir," she heard Melinda say.

Elizabeth stepped into the hall.

"I am back, however. Squire, I'm surprised to see you."

He smirked at her. "And not a pleasant surprise, or at least it won't be long. I've come to serve you legal notice that I'm taking over Kimberly, Miss High and Mighty."

Elizabeth blanched. Surely this was impossible!

"Lord Cade is in the next room. Let me summon him."

"Summon away, my lady, 'twill do you no good. I have in my pocket a notice of possession for delinquency in payments on the mortgage."

"May I see that, please?" Travis's quiet but determined voice sounded behind her.

"Certainly, my lord." The sneer in his voice was evident as he handed over a sheet of paper to Travis.

"Elizabeth, did you know anything about a mortgage?" he asked.

Elizabeth was as white as the document Travis studied.

"I have never heard of it, my lord. I cannot believe either my father would have forgotten to mention it, or that the Squire has never told me before."

"It does not matter, my dear. Please do not distress yourself. Even if it is legitimate, it is for a paltry amount."

"Your insulting me will do you no good, my lord," he scoffed. "I do not want the note paid. I refuse any payment on the grounds that too much time has lapsed since it was due. I have the right to take the property." His triumph was unmistakable as he stood, still in the hall, certain that he'd achieved at least one of his objectives. He'd have preferred to have Elizabeth along with the property, but if he couldn't have that, he'd at least ruin the proud bitch's life.

"My lord, is this possible?" Elizabeth went to Travis and placed both her hands on one of his arms.

"I will not let it be possible, my dear." He covered her hands with his. His tone was deadly, and Jack Crawley, standing in the background, was profoundly grateful he was not the Squire. He doubted if the man had any idea how relentless Travis could be when someone under his protection was threatened.

Bellamy did not lose his sneer.

"You talk big, my lord, but you can do nothing. Any debt this much in arrears can be called."

"I think not, Squire Bellamy. No notice was ever served. That in itself abrogates any seizure. I also have taken the precaution of investigating you. My man of business informs me of several dealings you would not want to be of widespread knowledge. Perhaps I will keep quiet about them, and perhaps I will not. In any case, you will leave this house instantly, never return, and never attempt to see Miss Drayton again."

The Squire had lost his smirk, but not his belligerence.

"I'm magistrate here, and what I say goes. I hereby serve notice of possession. I will give Miss Drayton three days to vacate. You can prove nothing against me in my own shire. I am the law here."

Elizabeth hung on every word, looking back and forth between the two men, and feeling hope well up along with a certainty that the Earl was the more powerful, and the most dangerous.

"You have a choice, Bellamy. Either leave immediately, or I will bodily throw you out and then take this to the courts in London. As a member of the House of Lords I have a great deal of influence, more than you can comprehend. If I lay before them that you tried to cheat and evict two orphans, you will likely end up in jail. Would you like me to also tell the story of the Widow Carden, and how you literally drove her from Stramshire? How she died shortly thereafter from poverty and heartbreak?"

Bellamy paled. He glared at the Earl with hatred.

"My man of business will call on you soon to redeem that note." Lord Travis's frigid tone had not changed. "Do not think to alter it in any way, as I am a very rapid reader and have the terms well memorized. Now leave."

Travis stepped forward, his stance that of a panther about to pounce.

Bellamy stepped back.

"You've not heard the last of this, my lord. Neither one of you has," he grated out, turning and stalking away.

He flung one last glance of unmitigated loathing at Elizabeth as he left. Next time he would make certain he got her alone. He wasn't through with that little bitch by any means.

Chapter Eight

ELIZABETH HEADED STRAIGHT for the Earl. He opened his arms and took her in, holding her to him, and kissing her hair. While he could not embrace her in the lover's way that he desired, he relished the feel of her supple body nestling against him, rejoicing she'd turned to him in trust.

He pried her face off his chest, and turned her face up to his.

"What is this, Elizabeth? You're trembling! Surely he did not frighten you that much! You must have known I would never permit him to take Kimberly!"

Her laugh was forced, but he appreciated the attempt.

"My lord, I know that in my heart, but he is so repellent! He quite alarmed me, I confess. I'm not sure there ever was such a mortgage. Surely papa would have mentioned it in those last weeks before he was dying."

"Signatures can be forged, of course," Travis said. "It might be useful to put a Bow Street runner onto investigating the Squire even more thoroughly. If we find he has unsavory connections with shady characters, it might be useful. In any case, it does not matter in the long run. I can deal with it, I assure you."

"I think I am more angry than anything else," mused Elizabeth. She had not moved from the shelter of his arms. Nothing had ever felt so absolutely right and natural.

She looked up at him, her face expectant. For a moment she thought she saw a flicker of fire deep in his eyes as he looked down at her. Then he hooded his gaze and slowly placed his arms at his sides. She had no choice but to step back, her face flaming at the thought that she'd practically invited him to kiss her!

He held himself rigid to fight the desire lancing through him. Thank God she was looking at the floor in embarrassment! She was so beautiful, and fit so perfectly in his arms. He would give a year of his life to claim the kiss they both desired. At least she hadn't spotted the huge bulge in his pants.

He took both her hands and kissed them.

"I want your happiness very much, Elizabeth. Do you believe that?"

"Of course, my lord," she murmured.

"Since you know I will do anything for you, will you do one small thing for me?" There was a half-teasing look on his face, but his tone was serious. "Could you bring yourself to call me Travis? I hate being 'my-lorded' all the time, and especially by you."

She found that easy to answer, and was grateful to the change of subject. He'd been Travis to her for some time. She'd been afraid she would slip in conversation and betray how often he was in her thoughts. So her consent was given with a smile. Melinda came to the door and stood looking at them.

"I don't know if you want more visitors or not, Miss Elizabeth. Vicar Carstairs is calling."

"How very nice." Elizabeth welcomed the distraction. "You will like him, you know, Travis. Do you know he came several times when you were ill, asking if he could help?"

Travis doubted very much that he would like him. Phillips had already told him of the calls, and that Richard had confided this was another man who wanted to marry Elizabeth.

"This is certainly our day for visitors," he said. "Please show him in, Melinda."

"He knows the way, Travis. And you'll like him, you know." Elizabeth beamed at the Earl.

A far too good-looking man, several years younger than Travis, with a shock of brown hair, a sturdy build, and a sweet smile, entered the room. Travis schooled his expression to one of neutrality.

"Elizabeth, Lord Cade. Your servant, sir." He bowed slightly and very correctly, his voice resonant and pleasing. Travis took note of the fact the Vicar felt free to use Elizabeth's first name. He'd already done some investigating of Carstairs. He knew he was the third son of the Earl of Darby. The first, the heir, was the well-respected Viscount Fitzwilliam, and the second had been on Wellington's staff and somewhat known to Travis. As a third son, with few options available, Robert Carstairs had chosen the church as a vocation. He'd always had a sympathetic nature, and a desire to help others. His parishioners were reputed to adore him.

He was admirable, as Elizabeth had said.

Travis could not warm up to him. After all, he doubtless still wanted to marry Elizabeth, and Travis did not like the idea of her being a vicar's wife, even though that vicar was nobly born. It was not an association he was going to promote. He'd make sure she married well, and this was not the man he wanted for her.

"My lord," said Carstairs, "I'm so very glad to finally meet you. I called several times when you were not able to receive me, but Elizabeth kept me informed of your progress."

"Did I tell you Robbie came several times during your illness? If I did not, I was remiss. He was most attentive."

Elizabeth sounded a little puzzled at the Earl's coolness. Travishad not missed the fact that she used a friendly diminutive of Carstairs' name.

Robbie directed his unaffected smile at both of them.

"I also wanted to tell you how wonderful I think it is that you are taking Elizabeth to London, my lord. She was entitled to a season and I hope doesn't regret too much she couldn't have one. London will be a wonderful opportunity for her. I think we must all be grateful to you."

Travis was astounded. For a lover to be appreciative of his chosen one leaving him was more than unselfish, it was insane. Was this man a saint?

He dropped a little of his animosity, and entered into the conversation more naturally. The vicar was not a saint, but he was a person who had been born with kinder instincts than most. He was not only personable, but eminently likeable, and Travis gradually thawed. Elizabeth was obviously fond of him, but although watching closely, he saw no signs of passion on her part.

Perhaps Carstairs was not so bad after all.

Travis had been worried for some time about Squire Bellamy, and this latest confrontation had alarmed him more than he wanted to admit. Perhaps he would talk with Carstairs privately, and elicit his help in keeping track of the villainous Squire.

When he finally left, Elizabeth turned to Travis in triumph.

"I knew you would like him. Everyone does!"

"You are a minx, Elizabeth. One shouldn't crow so much when proven right. I think I will have to give you a stern lesson in humility at the chess board tonight!"

She laughed and left him looking after her as she turned her graceful back and walked away. Both of them were achingly conscious their interlude of country intimacy was drawing to an end. Town life would be very different.

Travis told himself drearily that it was for the best.

Chapter Nine

ELIZABETH'S MIND KNEW well the time to leave for London was near. A letter received from Dr. Stratford, who ran the school Travis had attended before Eton, stated he would be pleased to accept Richard as a pupil.

Her heart was not quite reconciled to the departure, but Jack Crawley seemed firmly in command. Two ex-soldiers had already arrived as helpers. They'd gone immediately to work, and some of the tenant homes were being repaired. The manager's house was almost ready to receive Mrs. Crawley and their young son. Travis saw no need to tell Elizabeth that one of the new men was to sleep in the stables. Travis wanted to forestall any ideas Bellamy might have for making trouble.

"Elizabeth," said Travis one morning, as they rode out to check the new drainage system Crawley had in progress, "May I have your advice?"

Elizabeth was startled, but flattered. Up to now, the plans for London seemed to leave no room for her to have a say in any of the decisions.

"Of course, Travis. I can't imagine why a man of your wisdom needs advice."

"Stop that, you minx. Would you portray me as infallible or a tyrant?"

He grinned down at her and she smiled back sweetly.

"Very well, you won that exchange, Elizabeth. Now let's be serious. Have you lost some of your aversion to London, and would you like to give me a departure date you feel is acceptable?"

Again his consideration surprised and warmed her. It was true she was anticipating London more than she'd expected. She found herself daydreaming of shelves of unknown books, as well as seeing the museums and buildings. She shivered at the thought of seeing the dome of St. Paul's. And it's Whispering Gallery! And Westminster Abbey! Perhaps such splendid diversions would help her conquer what she feared the most, that Travis would be much less with her once they were away from Kimberly.

"Thank you, my lord, for your thoughtfulness. Would a week from today suit you?"

He smiled at her but shook his head.

"Only if you remember my name is Travis. And there is one other thing. I think it wise to have Phillips take Richard to Dr. Stratford's school. We can all ride together for almost the whole way, but I don't think I should undertake the extra riding to the school and then back to London. Richard, I think, likes Phillips well enough to make this a good plan. Again I want your opinion."

Elizabeth felt the usual wrench in her stomach at the thought of separation from Richard. Actually, this was an excellent plan. Richard admired and like Phillips, and would be well content to travel with him. The break would come in easier stages for them all.

"I think it a thoughtful plan, though I still find it hard to think of parting from him. I don't think Richard feels much of a struggle, but that's to be expected at his age. And Phillips's commonsense attitude is just right."

Travis did not let his sympathy show, but commented.

"Then I will send for the larger carriage. You and I and Aunt Lavinia can go in that with the bulk of the luggage. Richard and Phillips can take the small landau."

"And Palisades?"

"I will ride him alongside, and join you from time to time in the carriage."

Now that a date was set Elizabeth found her emotions in a surprising turmoil. There was regret at leaving Kimberly and separating from Richard, underlain with a bubbling excitement at actually seeing London. Mostly, she feared she wouldn't measure up to the standards of Travis' family. She was after all, little more than a country miss, with no town polish whatsoever.

She rode over the estate daily, spent a lot of time grooming Firebird and Blue Fire, and talking to them. Travis seemed intuitive, appearing at her side when she needed companionship, or letting her alone if she preferred solitude. He made no demands, but realized if she had a question or wanted companionship, he would be there to calm her unease. She loved knowing that if she looked for him, he was at her side. But would that be true in London?

When the carriage arrived from London, Richard was ecstatic. It came complete with four matched black horses, a coachman and a groom. The carriage itself was shiny black with deep maroon interiors, luxuriously padded squabs, and the distinctive crest of the Earls of Cade emblazoned on each side. Still, Richard didn't mind when was told he would be going in the smaller landau with Phillips. Just knowing his guardian owned such an elegant equipage seemed enough for him.

Elizabeth was delighted that the luxurious carriage would make the journey much easier for Aunt Lavinia, as well as Travis when he wished to join them. How splendid to travel in such style.

After resting the horses for two days, the group prepared to set out. Richard was almost dancing with excitement.

"I'm well content to ride in the landau, my lord," he said to Travis. "Phillips and I will have a wonderful time. Please don't think I am ungrateful if I ask that just for a short time I can join Elizabeth in the carriage. I have never ridden behind four horses before. It must be a treat."

"Of course you can, halfling. Your sister will welcome your company for some of the way. I'd planned it so myself. We'll stop at Redhill for lunch. Until we get there you may ride where you choose. I will be riding Palisades for at least that far. Perhaps for part of the time you might even want to ride with Coachman Peter. He's a wonder with the ribbons, and you can learn much by just watching him."

Richard was almost speechless with delight, but managed to stammer his thanks. Elizabeth, yet again, was suffused with admiration for this man who was so kind to everyone, and especially her brother. She could hardly keep herself from running to him and throwing her arms around him in gratitude. Only knowing he would not welcome it held her back. She schooled her features and hoped once again her embarrassing feelings didn't show.

As they set out through the softly rolling countryside, Elizabeth willed herself to enjoy the beauty. Hedgerows bloomed with wild roses and honeysuckle, and she reveled in the verdant countryside. The carriage was well sprung, and she was delightfully comfortable. She resolved to savor as much of the landscape as she could see. London wouldn't offer such natural beauty.

At the first rest stop, Travis dismounted from Palisades and laughed up at Richard perched by the coachman and chattering away.

"Come down, Richard, and stretch your legs like the rest of us. We are only halfway to Redhill, and if Peter can stand it, you can stay with him. Have a little compassion for him, however. He might not be used to such a chatterbox as you."

"Don' fret yourself, milord," Peter said with a grin. "I've got two boys myself, and I know all about how they love to talk. This young man makes me feel right at home."

Travis grinned and helped Aunt Lavinia out of the carriage to walk a little. Elizabeth had hopped out at the first opportunity, and was already well down the road. Merely looking at Travis tended to scatter her wits. His touch, even if he were just handing her down from the coach, shimmered her insides. London would doubtless be much more formal, and his touch would not affect her so mysteriously. A different atmosphere would lessen this hopeless attraction.

As she came back from stretching her legs, she found Travis delving into a big basket and passing out scones and lemonade. Before he took his own share, the Earl handed up refreshments to the coachman and the groom. They thanked him matter-of-factly, well used to his courtesy. No wonder his servants jumped to do his bidding.

The Earl joined them in the carriage for the next stretch as they passed through the small villages of Gatwick and Horly. Gray stone cottages nestled by the side of the road, many of them surrounded by late spring flowers, especially the wild geraniums that seemed to grow as prolifically as weeds.

Looking out, Travis murmured, "*Ah yet, ere I descend the grave, May I a small house and large garden have.*"

Elizabeth gave him a quizzical look. Did the responsibilities of the earldom weigh that heavily on him? Perhaps they did, since he'd not been bred to them. She knew he was responsible for at least three estates plus the London townhouse. So many people to have in one's care. She thought with chagrin of how much time he'd devoted to her problems. Yet she could not resist finishing the quotation.

"*And a few friends, and many books, both true, both wise and both delightful too.*"

Travis gave a shout of laughter.

"What a joy you are, Elizabeth. Indeed, who could ask for anything more than friends, books, and a garden? The size of the house is not really important. I must concentrate on the books and the friends. You are very good for me, my dear girl. Thank you."

His appreciation, uttered in such a tender tone, made her raise startled eyes to his. When his own fell, she changed the conversation.

"Tell me more about Sir Walter Scott's books," Elizabeth asked, and the talk centered on literature till they reached Redhill. The innkeeper was nearly overcome at seeing not one, but two crested carriages enter his courtyard, and immediately summoned his staff to do anything this noble party desired.

The lunch was undoubtedly the finest he could produce. Travis ate very little. Elizabeth noticed the pain lines were deepening again around his mouth and eyes. She lowered her eyes from his drawn face, and wished for his sake that the journey was over.

After lunch, Travis ushered Richard into the landau with Phillips, who immediately engaged him in debating the merits of a light vessel pulled by two horses, as against the larger carriage and the four matched blacks. This was a conversation that completely engaged Richard, and the leave-taking from the rest of the party went almost unnoticed, as the landau took one road, and the coach another. At the last moment Richard looked up and waved to them gaily. A mute Elizabeth watched him set off for a new life at Dr. Stratford's school. She would not be seeing him for some time, and he'd be changed when she did.

She turned to Travis in gratitude, her eyes brimming.

"That was neatly done, my lord. I am sure it was well planned between you and Phillips, and aimed at a minimum of fuss. Certainly it was a kind thing to let Richard go with no sisterly admonitions or tears. I thank you for us both."

Travis gazed at her in appreciation.

"Don't you know your own reaction is kindness itself? I was afraid you would blame me for being heartless. Most sisters would have, you know."

She gave him her dazzling smile. As usual, his heart flip-flopped in his chest.

"I hope I'm not like most women, my lord. I acquit you of anything but being truly thoughtful."

"Travis," he corrected.

He announced his intention of riding Palisades for the next stretch. Aunt Lavinia, whose chattering could be bothersome, fortunately took a nap. Elizabeth mused alone on her future and that of her brother. She concentrated on enjoying this peaceful interlude. She also worried that Travis' mother and sister would regard her as an imposition. Her thoughts jumped from one topic to another, and finally she just sat and wished Travis were there beside her.

Surely it would be easier to temper her attraction for Travis in the city, with its many distractions. They'd been thrown together far too much in the country. It would probably be an advantage to see less of him.

With a sigh, she settled in her corner and tried to doze.

Chapter Ten

AT CROYDON, TRAVIS again joined them in the carriage, but said little. He was obviously again in pain, so Elizabeth did not even try to force conversation. There was little to say. He would disdain sympathy, she knew well.

The road was now much busier, with wagons and carts as well as carriages jostling each other as they neared the city. Twilight was falling, but Elizabeth could still make out the majestic dome of St. Paul's cathedral. She thrilled at seeing one of the treasures she'd read about. The dignity of the cathedral's silhouette was all she had hoped. Most of the other buildings seemed enormous to her, and the noise exhilarating. Peddlers hawking their wares crowded the street, and as they neared the more fashionable parts of town, linkboys held torches high to light the way for the coaches of the peerage. Her delight was evident, and the Earl smiled in spite of his weariness and pain.

"I can't believe I am really in London," Elizabeth breathed.

"As I think I mentioned once before, Elizabeth, whatever else it might be, London is seldom boring."

She turned from the window, taking in his deepening fatigue.

"And is it always this noisy?"

"Sometimes much noisier. In the early morning, with the delivery men hurrying to supply the great houses, plus hawkers, street sweepers and errand boys, the noise is amazing."

"I find it invigorating. But don't the people who live here mind?"

"When I first arrived, I found it distressing. Now I think little of it, as I imagine most people come to do."

They had arrived in front of an impressive, four storied townhouse in Grosvenor Square. Torches flared on each side of the steps leading up to the double doors. As they slowed, a liveried footman hurried out to let down the steps, and another scurried up to solemnly hand out Aunt Lavinia and Elizabeth. Stepping down, Elizabeth saw a very proper butler holding open the front door, and she involuntarily turned toward Travis.

"Don't worry, Elizabeth," he whispered. "I won't let him eat you. He only likes the taste of young children, anyway."

He offered an arm to both ladies, and this time touching him was reassuring.

"Jamieson," he said to the stiffly postured man at the door. "I trust all is well. Will you please notify my lady mother that we are here? Could you ask cook for some light refreshment, and then I think we will all settle in for the night. Will you ask my mother to join us in the green parlor?"

Travis, limping badly, led the ladies to the parlor. Elizabeth had no time to look around before the door opened again for a diminutive lady, her white hair braided in a coronet around her head. Travis went to her as quickly as he could, and enveloped her in a hug that almost made her disappear.

"My lady mother, may I have the honor of presenting to you Miss Elizabeth Drayton and Lady Lavinia Cranston? We're fortunate they'll be our guests for some time."

Lady Rivington had been looking her son over since she had first come in. Her slight frown showed she'd not missed his pallor or his limp. However, she kissed his cheek and then moved at once to the ladies, holding out both her hands and grabbing Elizabeth's to keep her from sinking in a curtsey.

"You are both most welcome. Travis tells me not only will we have the honor of you as guests, but that you will help me with Claire's come-out. I cannot tell you how glad and grateful I am you're here."

She could not have been more gracious, but Elizabeth saw her glancing at Travis, a worried look on her delicate face. Elizabeth answered her, but felt like an interloper. Obviously his mother would not question him before guests.

"And where is Claire?" inquired the Earl. "I had thought she would be here to welcome us."

"It is entirely my fault she's not here, Travis. I insisted she go to a musical evening at the Branleighs, even though she begged to stay home. The Branleigh twins are also making their come-outs, and Claire seems to get along with them. She needs friends to help her through what she regards as an ordeal."

She went to her son and placed her hand on his arm.

"Mrs. Hadley will show the ladies to their rooms and they can freshen up before having a light supper. Then you can all settle down for an early night."

Elizabeth turned and let herself be led away, after one last glance at Travis. He was bent over his mother, and patting her hand. She thought however, he had reached the end of his endurance. She doubted if he appeared again that night.

Her room proved to be a delight. Pale blue damask drapes, antiques that were impressive but not ponderous, a large bay window piled with cushions that invited one to curl up and read. She'd buried her sorrow as she'd been forced to sell her own treasures, but rejoiced at being again surrounded by beauty, A silver bowl was filled with warm water, scented soap and fresh towels beside it. She splashed her travel weary face and hands, and put her hands up in despair to her disheveled hair. She was too tired to take down that heavy mane and do it up again properly, so she contented herself with coiling it as best she could at her neck. She knocked on Aunt Lavinia's door, and they descended together to find a sumptuous but light dinner, and Lady Rivington waiting for them.

The Earl did not appear, and it soon became obvious that in spite of her meticulous courtesy, his mother was very worried about him. The conversation was directed toward the guests, and all the ladies tried valiantly to keep it light and interesting. Travis was the one thing they did not mention.

As Elizabeth went up the stairs, she passed Phillips hurrying to a room two doors down from hers, and her heart sank as she saw the harried expression on his face.

She tried to put Travis out of her mind. She could do nothing to help him, and yet it was as if he were calling to her to come to him. She dealt almost automatically with the surprise of finding she'd been assigned a personal maid who had come to help her get ready for the night. It was a luxury she'd almost forgotten. Certainly having her hair brushed was an unbelievable comfort. But it didn't still her worries about Travis. How much was he suffering at this moment? Would Phillips be able to convince him to take some laudanum? Was this going to be as long and wicked an attack as the one at Kimberly?

She drifted off to a light sleep, exhausted from the trip, while one part of her kept listening for steps that might sound from Travis' room.

Chapter Eleven

ELIZABETH SLEPT LIGHTLY, and woke early, surprising the maid Susan, who was used to ladies sleeping much longer. She bustled into the room horrified that she had not been on hand immediately.

"My lady, let me get you some chocolate while you tell me what you would like me to bring you for breakfast. I am so sorry I was not ready for you this morning."

The little maid looked so appalled that Elizabeth hastened to reassure her.

"But I never eat breakfast in bed, Susan, so don't be concerned. Would you help me dress, and then show me to the breakfast room? I'm afraid I'll need guidance for a while as to which room is which."

She smiled so naturally that Susan appeared reassured. To Elizabeth, the luxury of a maid was a delight, and helped her forget for a moment her worries about Travis.

She entered the breakfast room to find Lady Rivington, seated alone, and picking at some coddled eggs on her plate. Elizabeth hadn't really expected Travis, but still she had hoped.

She helped herself to some eggs and toast, and let the butler pour her some coffee. She could find none of her enthusiasm of yesterday when first arriving in London. Lady Rivington was courtesy itself, but Elizabeth thought her smile a little forced. Finally she broached the subject on both their minds.

"Can you tell me, my lady, if Travis is having a bad spell? He had one at Kimberley and it quite frightened us all. Phillips says that one was unusually long. Has he told you anything about the Earl's condition now?"

Lady Rivington's face cleared a little.

"My dear, I am so glad you know about Travis' problem. If you had not I hesitated to know how much to tell you. I've spoken with Phillips, and he says this is a milder attack than the last one, which must have been the one you refer to. My poor son suffers dreadfully, as you must know, and there seems to be nothing we can do."

Elizabeth was somewhat reassured, but not enough to ease her anxiety.

"I'm sure you've had the best of doctors. I just can't reconcile myself to the fact they can do nothing."

"Nor I," answered his mother. "At times like this I wonder if we should take the chance of an operation. If they could find that piece of shot and extract it, he might be cured. But the thought of disturbing it and causing a worse situation keeps us from it. It's so hard to watch him go through these spells."

"He is incredibly brave, is he not?" Elizabeth said.

His mother smiled. "Phillips is delighted to tell anyone just how brave he's always been. When Phillips was his batman he worshipped him, but I think now, watching him deal with this horrible situation, he admires him even more."

"As we all do," said Elizabeth.

Something about her tone caused Lady Rivington to look at her more keenly.

Just then the door opened and a slight young girl whirled into the room.

"Claire, my love, let me present you to Miss Elizabeth Drayton. As you know, she is Travis' ward and our very welcome houseguest."

Claire's fair skin colored, and she swiftly curtsied to Elizabeth.

"Miss Drayton, we are so glad you are with us. But where is Travis? Did he not come with you?"

It was obvious she adored her brother.

Her mother slightly shook her head.

"He is in his room, my dear. I do not think this is a bad attack, but still he cannot join us this morning."

Claire looked devastated.

"And I was not here to welcome him when I could. How dreadful he must think me!"

"Claire, do not distress yourself. Travis went almost immediately to bed, and if you'd been here he would have striven to stay up with you. It was much better that you were *not* here."

"Is that really so, mama? You make me feel a little better."

Remembering her manners, she turned to Elizabeth.

"Miss Drayton, what a beginning to your visit. I am truly glad you are here. I long for a friend to help me through the thicket of society's rules."

Elizabeth offered her warmest smile.

"I hope very much to be your friend. In fact, I have had very few friends, since our farm was rather isolated, and I've longed for someone to confide in."

Claire's face lightened as her mother patted her hand.

"Then you forgive me for insisting you attend the Branleigh musicale, Claire?"

"Oh yes, mama. The twins are both very interested in music, Miss Drayton, and have an Austrian music master who was giving a small at-home concert. He was impressive, and I did enjoy it, but I would much rather have been here. I've missed Travis so much."

Turning to her mother she spoke in an impetuous manner. "Mama, do you think Miss Drayton and I could explore London a little, if we went together and took a maid? I have not done half the things I want, but together do you not think we could visit some of the museums and shops?"

Lady Rivington smiled. "Of course you can. I know today we must get a start on the proper clothing for Miss Drayton. Travis wrote me last week of what he wants her to have, and we might as well get started, since we'll likely not see him today."

Elizabeth looked at her in astonishment.

"But he has said nothing to me! And I truly do not have the funds for shopping, my lady."

"I think you need some suitable clothing if you are to accompany Claire. Think of it as a necessity in order to help us. And you are truly doing me the greatest favor."

Lady Rivington smiled at the look of dismay that crossed Elizabeth's transparent face.

"My dear," she said. "It is not so dreadful. We merely want you to feel at home in society. Trust me that it won't discommode Travis in the least, and indeed it will make things easier for us all. He very much wants you to enjoy London, and being with Claire. And I'm not of the constitution to be able to accompany Claire as much as I would like. You will be a blessing to me, you know."

Elizabeth saw no way out of this dilemma, unless she wanted to be a rude and obnoxiously stubborn guest. So she went along on the clothing expedition, and while still uneasy, had to admit she loved seeing the newest fashion books and patterns, and admiring the luxurious materials that the modiste draped around her.

Claire was ecstatic.

"You have such an elegant figure, Miss Drayton. So much more interesting than mine."

Elizabeth laughed. "If you mean it is fuller, you are correct, but I envy your slimness. And please, call me Elizabeth. I hope we will be the best of friends, and good friends use given names."

Claire colored with pleasure. "I would love to, Elizabeth," she said. "And of course you must call me Claire. Travis will be so pleased."

Travis had never left her thoughts, and Elizabeth was encouraged when Phillips came at dinnertime to bring greetings from his master, and the message he hoped to join them the next day. Suddenly her fears fell away. She could not see it, but she knew the sun was shining. Travis was not too stricken. She had been welcomed by Claire and Lady Rivington with a graciousness that staggered her. And while her pride much disliked the idea of having a new wardrobe supplied for her, she did think it might be pleasant to wear such lovely garments in front of Travis. It was really not such a bad idea. He might even cease to think of her as an obligation. Perhaps she would once again see that spark of fire that sometimes flared in his eyes.

Chapter Twelve

JACK CRAWLEY WAS A contented man. His wife and young daughter were now with him in the refurbished manager's house. He felt he had found a haven where he could well use his abilities in spite of his physical disability. Initially one or two of the new workers had looked askance at having a one-armed steward. His knowledge and the fairness of his discipline soon made them feel fortunate to be employed at Kimberly. All of the tenant's houses were being repaired, and they were eagerly filled as soon as they were habitable.

Crawley did not, however, relax. Above all things he wanted to do the best possible job for the Earl of Cade. The Earl had been most emphatic in warning him of Squire Bellamy. He'd stated he would try to do damage to Kimberly, but only in a manner where he could not be blamed. That probably meant he would hire someone of few scruples, and not a person known in the village.

Crawley tried to put himself in a villain's frame of mind, and thought about how injury could be done. Poisoning the wells would be one way, but it was chancy. Kimberly was blessed with many good wells, and all of them would have to be made undrinkable for that scheme to work. Burning the fields would be another, but Crawley did not think that a danger while the crops were so green. That left the possibility of setting fire to the main house or to the stables. He thought Travis had been most worried about the horses, since he had insisted one of the help always sleep in the stables. Injuring Firebird or Blue Fire would devastate Miss Drayton. So Hawkins and Bright, two very sturdy men, alternated weeks in sleeping near their stalls. In addition, Crawley went to the local pub to drink several pints with the owner. He made no insinuations, just promised that the pub keeper would be amply rewarded if he sent any information about a stranger in town asking questions.

About two weeks after everyone had left for London, Crawley got the word from the pub keeper. A stranger had shown up, asking questions about the whole village, but mainly about Kimberly. Crawley put both Hawkins and Bright in the stables for the next few nights. The new moon was only a sliver of light, and the darkness was ripe for an attempt at mischief.

Soon after midnight, one of the dogs started barking. Hawkins awakened and saw a wisp of smoke coming from the far corner of the stables. He'd been sleeping lightly, and immediately raced to the fire, shouting for Bright to clang the paddock bell.

Travis sat in London reading the report of that night.

"It was not too bad, my lord, as we were there at the beginning. The fire barely lit the sky. All the stable hands came running, throwing on their clothes as they came. Of course, the horses were terrified. Bright threw a rope halter on Blue Fire and rode him out. It was a brave act, and one I know you will want to congratulate him on. Hawkins led out Firebird, trembling, but not in the same panic as Blue Fire. It's a good thing Bright and Hawkins are rare strong men, or we couldn't have managed."

Travis smiled grimly at the realization that Crawley was taking no credit himself, although without his foresight they might not have been quite so lucky.

"Hawkins handed Firebird to me and dashed off looking for the arsonist. He saw him running away, but he was too far off to catch him. He says he's a slight man, and that's the way the pub keeper described the man who's been asking questions.

"The stables have been half burnt, but can be easily repaired. All the tenants are indignant and only too ready to pitch in, so it should not take long. Luckily, (more like foresight, thought Travis) *we had plenty of blankets and buckets of water ready to control the fire. I am convinced it was the work of Squire Bellamy, but, of course, can't prove it. Your lordship might want to have a Runner come down. I think the pub keeper could give him a good description of the stranger in town that night."*

Travis decided to put off telling Elizabeth for a little while. At least until the rebuilding was done. He did, however, mean to hunt down evidence. He'd certainly call in a Runner, but he also thought to consult Vicar Robbie Carstairs. Nothing must be allowed to happen to the horses that meant so much to Elizabeth.

Chapter Thirteen

ELIZABETH FOUND HERSELF much busier than she'd ever expected.

Claire invited everywhere, and felt more secure if Elizabeth were beside her. Sometimes Lady Rivington or Aunt Lavinia went along. Lady Rivington hadn't exaggerated when she had said her strength was limited. She was vivacious, but wilted quickly, and Elizabeth soon felt needed and appreciated. Watching Elizabeth's ease and animation of manner had just the effect on Claire that Travis desired.

Both Elizabeth and Travis badly missed their former hours together. Neither one thought of saying a word, and certainly not to each other.

One morning, Jamieson appeared at the doorway to the parlor where all the ladies were going through the latest fashion books.

"My lady," he said, handing some cards to Claire, "you have three visitors. I have put them in the green parlor."

When Elizabeth and Claire entered the parlor, they found two striking red heads, and one handsome blond man eyeing each other and obviously at a loss how to proceed, since they hadn't been introduced.

"Robbie," sang out Elizabeth, "how wonderful to see you! What are you doing in London and calling on Claire?"

Robbie flushed as only an embarrassed man can. "I did not know there were two beautiful young ladies in residence, and two more in the parlor. I handed in my card with instructions to deliver it to the young lady."

"You clunch," said Elizabeth, going up to him and lightly kissing him on the cheek. "Let me present you to Lady Claire Rivington, and the Branleigh sisters, Lady Melissa and Lady Amelia. Ladies, this is my dear friend, Vicar Carstairs."

The Branleigh twins were very alike, but not exactly. Melissa was slighter, taller, and more vivacious. Amelia was more serene, and of a sweeter disposition. Their dark auburn hair and more rounded figures made a lovely foil for Claire's fair and delicate beauty. Both of them had immediately registered the name Carstairs and assumed he was related to the Earl of Derby, and therefore acceptable. Claire knew only that he was the most appealing man she'd ever seen. She said nothing, but her eyes seemed unable to move from his fine-looking face.

Elizabeth was highly amused at the obvious and universal approval of her friend.

"But what are you doing here, Robbie? It's most unlike you to be in London, especially during the season."

"My mother commanded my presence, Elizabeth. She is not feeling well and needed one of her sons around her. Since my brothers are temporarily not available, she sent for me. I am most happy to oblige, of course, and especially since my father sent a young curate to temporarily take my place."

Elizabeth's eyebrows raised a little at this explanation. She privately thought that having her very handsome son in London during the season had little to do with the Countess' state of health. Exposing him to beautiful females was more important. In any case, she was delighted to see him. She felt his proposals of marriage stemmed a great deal from the fact that he was a genuinely caring person, who responded to anyone in a difficult situation. She knew he had a sincere admiration for her, but not an abiding love. She had never felt it enough basis for marriage, even though it would have solved many of her financial problems.

All three of the young ladies looked at Robbie with admiration. Elizabeth almost felt like a chaperone as she watched Amelia and Melissa attempting to sound him out.

"Will your stay in London be long, Mr. Carstairs? How wonderful if you could see some of the sights with us!"

This astonishingly came from Claire, who was usually reticent when others were present.

Robbie's smile gave no doubt of his admiration of her delicate beauty.

"I will certainly be here for a while, Lady Claire. My mother insists I do not stay in her pocket, but get around while I am here. I am a dutiful son, so I shall make the best of following her dictates. I would love to join you at any time you invite me."

This was said with his usual charming smile. Elizabeth thought he had done very well. Everyone now knew he was a vicar, yet both he and his family were in favor of his attending the appropriate social functions.

Just then Lady Rivington entered the parlor. Elizabeth immediately presented Robbie, who bowed low over her hand.

"How nice to meet you, Mr. Carstairs. I know your mama well. I trust she is in good health?"

"Not quite as well as I would like, my lady, but I hope she will soon be in fine fettle. She sent her greetings, and charged me to tell you she hopes to call on you soon. I take it you've not been long in London this season?"

"And not for several seasons," said Lady Rivington. "We are newly arrived to present Claire to society, along with Elizabeth."

"Oh no, madam," cried Elizabeth. "We are all eager to present Claire, that's true, but I am merely here to assist."

Lady Rivington smiled. "You will not need a formal presentation, my dear. But enough of that. Are you all going to the concert tonight, as we are?"

The twins, with their genuine interest in music, were soon chattering about how thrilled they were to be invited to the private concert where Angelica Catalini was to sing. Catalini was a slight, dark woman with a large and beautiful voice, and she had captured even the most blasé of sophisticates in London

Travis entered in time to hear them all agree to meet at the musicale.

"Carstairs!" he exclaimed. "I did not know you were in London."

Robbie grinned at him. "I am newly arrived, my lord."

"You are welcome," said Travis, in such a sincere and solemn tone that Elizabeth stared at him.

"You four must be the loveliest quartet in all of London." Travis cast his devastating smile on all of them.

He kissed his sister on the cheek. Elizabeth smiled. She privately thought the Branleigh girls were shrewd enough to appreciate the picture they made when grouped with Claire. Since Claire benefited from the friendship, Elizabeth did not voice her reservations. Without companions to bolster her, Claire tended to retreat behind a wall of shyness.

All expressed delight when Travis stated he would escort them to the musicale. She'd always thought him handsome, and the sight of him in evening attire made Elizabeth glow with a warmth that flushed her cheeks. Her heart jolted with the disturbing rhythm only he could produce. He was dressed all in black, with white lace spilling at his neck and wrists, and a single large ruby on his elegant hands. She had long thought him the epitome of manliness, but in her eyes no one could equal him this night.

It was a gay party, with Robbie joining them as soon as they arrived. The Branleigh twins immediately swarmed over to him, and he gave Claire and Elizabeth a rueful glance as they led him off to meet some of the other guests.

More than once Travis found himself watching Elizabeth more than the singer. She was completely absorbed in the music, and he doubted if she even knew where she was. For once he could look at her to his heart's content. He caught his mother looking at him one such time, and smiled sweetly at her. She knew him far too well to be in any doubt of his feelings, but he knew she'd never betray him. She also did not expect him to discuss his emotions.

At the end of the concert, Travis enlisted help from Robbie, and set off to find refreshments for the ladies. As he looked around for Claire, he stiffened. Elizabeth quickly followed his glance. Claire and the twins were surrounded by several men, and attention was being paid equally to them all. She could see no objection.

She watched more closely. One of them was broad shouldered and had an athletic air. The second wore a bright pink waistcoat with large gold buttons that were positively dazzling. The third, slightly older with a dissipated face, seemed amused by the chatterbox twins, but kept his eyes on Claire.

"Do you know those gentlemen?" she asked Lady Rivington.

"The attractive young man in dark green is Lord Gerald Stokely, younger son of the Earl of Avon. The fashionable is Sir Roger Stanton, a baronet. But I do not know the other."

She turned to her son, who had a rather fixed look on his face.

"I do know him," Travis stated in a coldly neutral tone. "And I cannot like him as an acquaintance for Claire. He is Reginald Forbush, the nephew of the Duke of Caldwell. He is, however, very far down the line in succession for the title, and has little prospects of his own. While his lack of title does not bother me, his mode of life does. He is deep in dun territory. Reportedly his uncle has refused to frank him any further. He is reputedly looking for an heiress to rescue him."

Elizabeth looked at him in surprise. Travis never repeated gossip, nor even listened to it. Such a detailed portrayal could only be deliberate. He had put them on notice. Evidently he wanted them all to help guard Claire.

Robbie, who'd been listening intensely, smiled and turned to Elizabeth and Lady Rivington.

"With your permission, ladies, I will leave you to your refreshments and join the group around the young ladies. Do you not agree that the more gentlemen attending them, the more dazzling their success?" With a smile and a bow he made his way across the room.

Elizabeth's thoughts were turned around. She had not considered the fact that Claire would have a considerable dowry as the sister to the Earl of Cade. She'd already learned Lady Rivington was simply not capable of attending every social function with Claire. Perhaps this was another way she could be of use to Travis.

The thought gave her great satisfaction. Now if only Travis would stop staring so grimly across the room. His displeasure was beginning to be noticeable, at least to her.

Watching him, Elizabeth was startled to see his expression completely change, and his face light with pleasure. As she looked on, a handsome older man came up to him and enthusiastically shook his hand. On second glance, he was still handsome, but not that much older. His shock of prematurely gray contrasted with his youthful face and vigorous appearance. For some reason, this seemed to give him a rather impish air, as if he were a child playing at being grownup. There was nothing childish, however, about the appreciative glance he gave Elizabeth. He bent low over each of the lady's hands, but Travis did not miss the extra few seconds his lips lingered on Elizabeth's.

"Madam," Travis said with evident enjoyment, "you have often heard me speak of David Lansdowne, the Viscount Kingsley. This is the rascal who served with me in much of the Peninsular campaign. Lady Lavinia, and Miss Drayton, may I present one of my dearest friends. The fact that he's a rogue should never deter you from enjoying his company. Do not, however, believe a word he says about me."

"What an astonishing introduction, Travis," said his smiling mother.

"Do not be concerned, Lady Rivington. Travis is only telling the truth when he names me a rascal, and I've never held honesty against any man. I do, however, beg you to give me a chance to show what a really fine fellow I can be."

Kingsley's smile would have charmed anyone, and none of the ladies proved to be an exception. Both men grinned, and Elizabeth decided this was a perfect opportunity to find out more about Travis. This genial gentleman was just who she had been looking for.

"Then you can prove how fine you are by answering some questions. I know better than to ask Lord Cade to speak much of the war, but since you mentioned the Peninsular campaign, were you together from the start? Did you serve in the same regiment?"

The Viscount smiled down at her. "Yes to both of those questions. Travis and I were together from the very beginning, when Wellington picked us to help map the terrain of Portugal. We worked together for months. Neither side had maps. Wellington's ability to plan campaigns based on accurate maps gave us an advantage we sorely needed."

As usual, Travis interrupted any talk of the war.

"But you have not told me why you are in London, David. Are you on leave? If so, I hope it is a long one, and we can spend much time together."

David spoke a little less exuberantly.

"I've decided to sell out my commission. My father was injured when he was thrown from his horse, and is presently confined to his room. I'm needed here at home."

"I'm very sorry for the reason, but not that you are selling out. I've lived in dread of seeing your name on the casualty lists. I'm heartily glad to welcome you to London."

"And I'm more than pleased to see you enjoying life again. My last visit with you at the hospital was not quite so reassuring!"

It was obvious Kingsley wanted to ask about Travis' health, but Travis forestalled him with questions about Brandy, David's stallion that had been with him for most of the campaign. Elizabeth was content to let the talk veer to horses, and entered in with stories of Firebird and Blue Fire that clearly showed her knowledge of good horseflesh. She could have done nothing to glue Kingsley more closely to her side. Travis watched, a mechanical smile on his face, as his best friend fell under her spell. Damn. He'd have a hard time thinking of a reason why she shouldn't accept David.

Why hadn't David seen Claire first, as that was a match he could heartily endorse. He was far from ready to hand Elizabeth over to a man.

Any man.

Chapter Fourteen

THE INHABITANTS OF Travis' house held very different thoughts running through their minds, and they were all busily thinking them.

Elizabeth thought she was probably an idiot. She had several men paying attention to her last night, and one of them Lord Kingsley, was outstandingly attractive, and signified in little ways that he found her equally so. Why then this feeling of unease? She decided to go seek out Claire and get her reaction to the evening and to the men she had met.

"They were all very agreeable, Elizabeth," Claire said "Something about Mr. Forbush made me uneasy, though."

"Did you have a pick? Perhaps the handsome Viscount Kingsley?"

"No, he was most amusing. But I think I felt most at home with Mr. Carstairs. He was so adept at rescuing me from Mr. Forbush, and did it in such an unpretentious manner. But I think you've talked of him before, and that he is your friend in a special way, is he not?"

Surprised, Elizabeth had not realized until now that talking about how Robbie had befriended her at her father's death had given that impression.

"We are very old and good friends, it's true. At one time he had an interest in me, but I think it was just that when he first came to Stamshire he was lonely, and I was the only young person around to help make it more agreeable. It's not important at all. In the meantime, you and the twins are the toast of the season, and you'll have your pick of men. Robbie will be only one of many."

"I'll remember what you say, Elizabeth. But I'm still frightened of having a season. Last night was pleasant, but night after night of seeing the same faces seems so pointless. Sometimes I don't really like all the people, and of course cannot do anything but simper and be polite. And I'd dearly like more time to myself. I'm not the type to enjoy constantly going to parties."

She gave a little shudder, and Elizabeth suspected she was remembering Forbush and his forward attitude.

"The twins are enjoyable to be with, are they not? I'll wager they have no doubts about having a season. Seldom have I seen a more exuberant pair!"

Claire's smile was genuine. "They do carry on, don't they? But much as I enjoy them, I can't agree with them. Each of them is only thinking of catching a husband."

"Are you saying you do not desire a husband?" Elizabeth said, half jokingly, and half anxious to hear Claire's answer.

"Oh, of course I do. What girl does not? But I don't think having a title is the basis for choosing. Missy and Amelia won't care if their future husband is old and ugly, as long as he is at least an Earl, and preferably a Duke or Marquis!"

"And you don't agree? For shame, Claire!"

Claire laughed. "Elizabeth, you're bamming me! I know you'll want a husband to share your every thought, as well as one you love as dearly as he loves you. Don't try to tell me differently."

Elizabeth walked over and kissed her quickly on the cheek.

"Of course not, love. I'm so glad I don't have to worry about you taking a wrong turning. You know society would not agree with either one of us."

Claire looked confused.

"But, Elizabeth, you are so lovely and intelligent, surely you can have any man you want. You converse with anyone easily, and everyone admires you. I think you'll have your pick more than I!"

Elizabeth did not disabuse her of the notion. She knew that without a dowry she had little chance of marrying well, but that didn't concern her. What did concern her were her feelings for Travis. She fervently hoped no one guessed how her whole existence was built around the times she was with him. It would be humiliating if anyone suspected.

She doubted she would ever marry. She knew Travis was out of her reach, but she could not imagine another man who would ever make her feel as he does. Unless someone appeared whose very presence made her quake, whose every inadvertent touch made her tremble, she was lost to what would eventually become memories of him. She'd not thought it possible to feel this deeply for anyone. He was kindness itself, and she owed him so much. Not just a monetary debt, as she trusted she could someday repay all his investment.

He had taught her what a man could be. And in doing so he had ruined her for any other man.

TRAVIS THOUGHT HE WAS becoming a besotted lunatic. It had been brought home to him last night, when he had seen that David was obviously smitten. He had felt so fiercely proprietary about Elizabeth that he had almost turned on his best friend, merely for kissing her hand a little too enthusiastically. She was his woman, and no one else could touch her. That had been his instinctive reaction, and it horrified him. He closed his eyes against the shaft of longing that struck through him.

He could never think of marriage. How could he, when he did not know when the next attack would be the one that left him paralyzed? His head in his hands, he sat silently. He'd best get himself under control, and help her find a husband worthy of her.

Claire thought that perhaps having a season was not as bad as she had expected. The morning following the concert found flowers delivered for Claire from Sir Stanford, Lord Stokely, and Reginald Forbush, as well as a large bouquet for Elizabeth from Lord Kingsley. Robbie's tributes were imaginative, daffodils to Elizabeth, and lilacs to Claire. Elizabeth noted that Claire took only the lilacs up to her room.

Lord Stokely invited Claire for a ride in Hyde Park, and Robbie engaged Elizabeth. Both men arrived at the same time, and Stokley's low-slung carriage, with the Avon crest on both doors, complete with two grooms, was most impressive.

The men went to the door to find both ladies waiting for them. Claire was smiling in innocent delight.

"Lord Stokely, your carriage is magnificent. It is large enough we will all fit in. Don't you think it a famous idea if we join parties?"

Lord Stokely was too well bred to do anything but assent, and so they all set out. This was not at all Elizabeth's idea of an enjoyable outing. She preferred riding neck-or-nothing across the fields. Riding sedately along Rotten Row, with all the other carriages slowing to try to sniff out a new item of gossip, did not amuse her.

She looked at Robbie, intending to quietly voice her thoughts, which she felt he'd agree with. She found him staring at Claire and her partner. Stokely had paid Claire the supreme compliment of turning the horses over to one of the grooms, so he could better talk with her.

Suddenly Stokely turned to Robbie. "You are recent to town, are you not, Carstairs? And I understand a member of the clergy. Have activities lured you here, or is it the chance of saving some lost soul?"

The sneer in his voice, although slight, was unmistakable.

Claire and Elizabeth both looked at him with indignation. This was not even passably courteous.

Robbie answered in his usual soft manner.

"My activities are not the same as yours, my lord, but some of them might overlap. I spent two hours today boxing with Gentleman Jackson. Do you frequent his salon?"

Claire looked at him with admiration. He'd just served notice that he was a very fit athlete, as Jackson personally sparred with very few. He had delivered a very polite set down.

Stokely turned crimson, and Elizabeth rushed into the conversation.

"Why on earth do they call this Rotten Row? Tis a very strange name for a popular road through the park."

Stokely had the grace to seize upon the new topic, and the danger point passed.

"It's surely not much test of a good team, but it's the fashionable place to be at five o'clock of an afternoon."

"I know you are much admired for your driving expertise. Is it true you won a bet by driving to Ipswich in less than five hours?"

Elizabeth turned her most admiring look on him, and it seemed to work. He began to elaborate on riding horseback as against driving a carriage, and everybody joined in. Elizabeth had been watching Claire closely. She did not think Stokely's wealth or title had made the least impression on the girl. She and Robbie were exchanging a good many glances.

Elizabeth didn't know whether to be amused or worried. What would Travis think if his sister decided she preferred a vicar to all the titled gentlemen bound to be pursuing her? A topic perhaps worth pursuing the next time she talked with him.

Lately, she'd had little chance to speak to Travis privately. It was almost as if he were trying to avoid being alone with her. She was beginning to suspect that was indeed the case. She couldn't in the slightest understand it. He was as kind as ever when she saw him, but did not see him often. As far as she knew, she'd done nothing to offend him. The topic gnawed her further even while she dressed to go to the opera that night.

All the ladies and Travis were in the Cade box at the Opera House on Haymarket Street. The first act of Don Giovanni had been brilliant, and Elizabeth had lost herself completely in the lovely, lilting strains. She suddenly felt her hand taken gently by Travis.

"Elizabeth, come back to us. You have completely gone away."

Elizabeth came to with a start, and a *frisson* ran through her as Travis continued to hold her hand. It was no wonder, she thought. He was so handsome, impeccably garbed in his usual black evening attire, with a huge pearl pin securing his cravat as his only ornament. Elizabeth caught her breath. His elegant looks made her insides simmer. Perhaps he felt her tremor, for he dropped her hand and moved away, saying he would fetch the ladies some lemonade.

Lord Kingsley entered the box, followed closely by Lord Stokely, Sir Stanton, and Reginald Forbush. Kingsley crossed to Elizabeth, while Forbush merely nodded to everyone and then leaned against the wall of the box, arms akimbo.

Sir Stanton was dressed not in the usual evening attire, but in white breeches and a silver striped waistcoat. While it would have looked outrageous on anyone else, he took at the attention as his due and end preened a bit. Stokely and Stanton made a game of vying for Claire's notice, and soon had her laughing, while Kingsley headed straight for Elizabeth.

"You are in looks tonight, Miss Drayton."

She flushed a little at the sincerity in his voice, and thanked him.

"I couldn't help noting during the first act how engrossed you were. Are you a true opera enthusiast then?"

"No, my lord. I've had little experience of opera, but I find this absolutely enchanting."

She wished ladies were allowed to issue compliments as easily as the male of the species, as she thought him a striking figure, with his shock of thick gray hair and his air of crackling vitality. She moved over to give him a place between herself and Claire.

Forbush, after not saying a word, heaved himself away from the wall and left. He had kept his eyes fixed intently on Claire. The atmosphere lightened when he left, as they all seemed more relaxed.

At the end of the intermission, Stokely and Stanton bowed themselves out, but Kingsley stayed. He was so affable, and distributed his conversation around so equally, that all the ladies enjoyed his company. Travis alone did not respond.

Elizabeth noticed his silence, and turned to try to draw him out. She found him with his head thrown back and his eyes closed, and fresh pain lines etched on his face. She'd tried to ignore the difficulty he'd had with the steep stairs in the Opera House. Alarmed, she tapped Kingsley's arm and motioned with her head to draw his attention to Travis.

David gave one look at his friend and recognized the problem. He raised his eyebrows at Elizabeth, who motioned him to go. Just before the next intermission, he drew Travis to his feet and wrapped his arm firmly around his shoulders. Laughing and chatting, David led him away. To a casual observer they would appear only as two very good friends immersed in a private conversation.

The ladies silently watched the men leave. They did not worry about getting home unescorted, as the coachman was reliable.

None of them heard much of the remaining arias, and Elizabeth didn't hear a note.

Chapter Fifteen

THE LAST ACT OF THE opera seemed interminable, but they endured it, knowing it would draw too much attention if they left early. The ride home was silent, and Elizabeth went quickly to her room on reaching the house. She lingered a while at Travis' door, but could hear nothing. Dispirited, she went to bed, but sleep did not come easily. She kept listening for sounds of his pacing, until she finally fell into an uneasy sleep.

The next day passed uneventfully, with the whole household striving for normalcy, and all of them waiting, waiting, for some word from Phillips. He finally appeared in the late afternoon, looking rather haggard as if he had had little sleep. He announced the Earl had had a mild setback, but it was nothing to worry about, and that his master wanted the women of his household reassured.

Elizabeth was not. She went through the motions of the day, but could think of nothing but Travis. His inherent strength had carried him through so far, but how long could he resist these insidious attacks? How could he hope for any future happiness, when this demonic infirmity could strike without warning? She longed to share his trials, but knew he wouldn't allow it. If she could only go to him and declare her feelings, telling him she didn't care in the slightest about anything but him and easing his burden! She suspected that would not only distress him, but that he would reject such sentiments out of hand.

Late that night, after tossing restlessly in her bed, she determined to go to him and check his condition for herself. Perhaps this time there was something she could do. Putting a robe over her night rail, she padded down to his room. Phillips answered her gentle knock.

"Miss Drayton." Phillips looked exhausted as if he had been up ever since the night before, which was probably the case.

"Phillips, may I please come in? I need to know for myself that Lord Cade is alright."

"Miss Drayton, he is not alright, but he is much better. He is sleeping now. He would not want you in the room, however. You know his pride."

Phillips stood holding the door only partially open, so she could not see in.

"You look worn to the socket, Phillips. Would you at least allow me to spell you off for a while? I'm sure you have been up a very long time, and I am perfectly rested. If he is sleeping, may I not sit with him? I promise to call you if there is any change."

Phillips was tempted. He'd been with the Earl for about thirty hours now, and was indeed worn out. He knew the Earl valued Miss Drayton highly, and that the feeling was returned.

Elizabeth saw the struggle of his thoughts reflected in his face.

"Please, Phillips. It would make me feel so much better, and cannot hurt him."

Phillips gave a short laugh. "Indeed, I don't think anything could hurt him right now. This is one time I was able to get a powerful amount of brandy down him. It's eased the pain so that he probably won't wake for hours."

"Then what does it matter who is by him? Go get some rest, and I'll be happy to sit with him."

Phillips hesitated a little longer. His master was deeply asleep; in fact, he was thoroughly foxed, as he did not normally drink much. Perhaps letting Miss Drayton watch for an hour or two wasn't a bad idea. He could be back in plenty of time before the Earl awoke, and would be better for a little rest.

Elizabeth saw his decision in his eyes, and lowered her own, so he would know the jubilance she felt. To sit with Travis, watching over him, was all she wanted for the present. He would never know, and she could love and admire him as she couldn't do when surrounded by his family.

Phillips opened the door. Elizabeth cast one glance at Travis, and saw he was indeed asleep. She longed to go to him and stroke the hair that fell over his eyes, but attempted only a cursory look. She certainly wouldn't give Phillips a chance to change his mind.

"Here, miss. Take this blanket and wrap up in it in the big chair. You don't look too warm to me."

Elizabeth flushed. Indeed, she wasn't. She had forgotten that both the robe and the night rail were thin, and she took the blanket gratefully.

Phillips turned toward the door.

"I think you're right, miss. I need spelled a little. I thank you, and I'll be back in an hour or so."

Elizabeth knew she would be content to sit the rest of the night, watching Travis breathe.

"I'm perfectly fine, Phillips. I can doze in this chair. It's really very comfortable."

She flashed him a smile that quelled his doubts. Miss Drayton was such an exceptional lady. He'd not mind at all if she could talk the Earl into marriage.

Elizabeth curled up in the chair and let her eyes feast on Travis. Asleep, the pain lines were diminished, and he seemed younger. His prominent cheekbones had always attracted her, showcasing his strength of character. His black hair was irresistibly tousled. In repose, his lips showed the inherent sensuality that his sternness sometimes hid. She thought she would be content to look at him for as long as Phillips chose to rest.

As she watched, he began to move a little. He shifted restlessly, then turned on one side. Suddenly one arm threw off his blankets as he muttered incoherently and rolled on his back.

Elizabeth went to the bedside and tried to reach the blanket to cover him, but it was on the far side. She sat down carefully so as not to further disturb him, and stretched over him to catch the edge of the blanket.

She had no time for anything but a small gasp, when Travis grabbed her body to his, holding her tightly with both arms.

"Elizabeth," he mumbled. "Beautiful, beautiful Elizabeth."

Their faces only a few inches apart, Elizabeth could see that his eyes were not quite focused, but they were lit by a fire which she'd never seen. She stared at him, knowing that this was but a mirror of the flame deep within her own pulsing body. It seemed so right to her to be held by this man. She knew she should move, or at least say something to get his attention. She felt the warmth that always swirled through her at his touch grow hotter, and she reveled in the mysterious feelings he aroused. If this was wrong, she did not want to set it right.

Travis pulled her face down for a drugging kiss. She finally had his mouth, and it was everything she'd hoped it would be. In fact, the reality so far surpassed her innocent imaginings that she took a deep breath before coming back for more. Travis obliged willingly, and she drowned in the seductive passion that was so new and enticing. His two-day-old beard was rough against her face, but she thought only of his masculine strength, and his scent, a combination of male, Travis and brandy.

He parted her lips with a velvet tongue and plundered her mouth, tasting her as if she were a delectable dish he'd long desired. She was startled at his invasion, but soon tentatively put the tip of her tongue in his mouth, to his seeming delight. He began to murmur to her, soothing and delightful words of admiration. He kissed every inch of her face, caressing her body at the same time, his clever hands moving incessantly over her.

Suddenly, she realized he had switched to kissing her neck and bare arms. She had no idea how he had so adeptly removed her robe, but she liked being kissed everywhere. She thought hazily that this was not as new to him as it was to her, but that didn't matter. As long as he held her so lovingly, nothing could bother her. His caresses sent little bolts of pleasure through her body, wishing he would never stop. He kissed and caressed her tightened breasts, and heat pooled in the lower part of her body, where all of her senses seemed to be suddenly concentrated.

Just then Travis made a quick movement and she found herself flipped on her back, pinned under him while he reared over her and continued caressing her with his lips and hands.

She had no doubts at all. This was Travis, and whatever he wanted she'd be honored to give him. Even when she felt his erection, hot and heavy against her stomach, she didn't hesitate. She had seen animals mate, and knew the basics, but did not know quite how it applied to humans. She felt him raise her night rail to her waist, and thought she was about to find out. Her only emotions were a feeling of almost unbearable pleasure, and of gratitude.

Travis kept up his low murmuring, assuring her of her beauty and how much he desired her. Suddenly he placed his sex at her entrance, and with one powerful thrust joined his body to hers. She felt no particular pain, but the tightness was uncomfortable. He waited a moment, breathing heavily, and then began to move inside her.

At first Elizabeth could only marvel at how her body seemed to stretch to accommodate him. The discomfort vanished, and she was flooded with sensation. She felt her very bones melt into his, and thought how perfectly their bodies fit together. Pleasure seemed to radiate from an unknown spot between her legs, and she strained toward something she did not understand. Just as her pleasure started to mount, he gave several deep thrusts, and then collapsed against her. Stunned at first, she kept waiting for the enjoyment to resume. Then, as his heavy body lay inertly on her, she realized that her time of being loved was over.

Travis rolled off her and onto his side, saying her name once again, before his eyes closed and he was deep in a passion and whisky induced sleep.

Elizabeth lay there, not entirely discontented, but puzzled. How could she be discontented when she had tasted the joys of physical union with the man she loved? If she had her way it would not be the last time they came together. She was sure she had a great deal more to learn! In the meantime, she'd better get out of bed and into the chair before Phillips reappeared.

Chapter Sixteen

SHE WANTED TO SPEND a moment looking out at the beautiful night, gathering her thoughts, but she did not want to chill Travis. Piling her own blanket on him, she opened the window and let the breezes blow briefly in. The sky was lit by a full moon, with clouds drifting over it. Since she knew it was a night she would always remember, she was elated it was such a beautiful one. How fortunate, to live in such a glorious world, and one that contained Travis!

By the time Phillips appeared, she'd long been in her chair, wrapped up again, but not asleep. What had just happened was too momentous and thrilling to even think of sleep. She wanted to savor every minute of it. It might be a long time before she could convince Travis to make love to her again. She had no illusions that anything but the brandy had weakened his control. But she knew he'd enjoyed it from the way his heart had thudded against hers as he lay on her, and from the peaceful look on his face as he slept.

What would he say when he wakened? Would he remember? She didn't know whether to hope he did, or to pray he had no recollection. On the whole, she thought it might be better if he forgot. She was in his care, and knowing his sense of honor, it would devastate him to know he had taken her virginity. Telling him she'd encouraged him might not matter.

Even as she mulled over her marvelous evening, she decided to keep him from any suspicion if she could without compromising her honesty. When Phillips reappeared, she told him all was well, pretended to be sleepy, and slipped out quietly.

Travis awakened in the morning, a smile on his face. He felt unusually well, and decided brandy as a curative wasn't a bad idea. The pain in his leg had subsided to a dull ache, and he had a slight brandy headache, but his spirits were higher than normal.

He'd had the most marvelous dream. Elizabeth had come to him and willingly given him her glorious body. As he lay there, his arms behind his head, he went over the details of the dream. Usually he couldn't remember so much when he dreamt. He could practically see her and taste her! What a lovely dream it was!

"Good morning, my lord Captain," said Phillips. "From the look on your face I would guess this bout is over. You didn't have it too bad, praise Gawd."

"You look in good shape too, Phillips." Travis smiled. "Did you manage to catch a little sleep last night too? I know you did not the night before."

"We can both thank Miss Elizabeth for that. She sat with you a while so I could sleep without worrying about you. That is one fine lady, Captain."

Travis stilled. He heard nothing but that Elizabeth had indeed been in the room with him.

"And how long did she stay, Phillips?" he asked. Surely he was imagining there could be a connection to his vivid dream.

"About two hours, milord." Phillips looked anxious. Perhaps he had been wrong to be gone so long, but with the captain passed out it had not seemed improper. And Miss Elizabeth had been so insistent.

Travis said nothing, but his mind was scurrying. Surely he could not have truly done what his memory told him he might have. His love for Elizabeth simply would not have permitted him to desecrate her in that manner.

"Will you get my breakfast now? I find I am rather hungry."

"With pleasure, my lord." Phillips was indeed delighted to have him actually ask for food. He scurried off, determined to bring back everything his master might want.

As soon as Phillips left Travis swung back the covers. He was deeply disturbed at even the suspicion that his dreams might be real. He did not ever remember being able to recollect another dream in such detail. He could almost feel the soft texture of Elizabeth's skin, and see the lovely arch of her neck as it sloped into her shoulders. He thought he knew how to quell his fears. There was no doubt in his mind that Elizabeth was a virgin. If he had taken her there would be bloodstains on the sheets; it was as simple as that.

With the covers back he stared down at the bed. There were some stains, but no blood. He let out a long, slow breath of relief. The brandy had merely helped him to have the most pleasurable dream he'd ever enjoyed. He could face Elizabeth when he saw her, and hopefully put the dream out of his mind. It simply would not do to dwell on its delights. Still, it had been an amazing experience. He decided on a bath and then going downstairs as soon as possible. He wanted to see Elizabeth. His suspicions were mostly, but not completely, quelled. All the evidence seemed to bear out what he hoped was true, he still wanted to look into Elizabeth's transparent eyes.

Elizabeth had spent a night of little sleep, in a state of almost exultation. She knew now that Travis at least desired her, even though it might not count as love. He might have responded physically to any woman he found in his bed, but he had fallen asleep with her name on his lips.

But more and more she felt he must not know what had happened between them. So she was hesitant about meeting him. Deciding that unless he directly put the question to her, she could turn aside any misgivings. And perhaps he would have none. Perhaps he'd fallen into such a deep sleep that he'd have no memory of what had occurred.

She was sitting in the morning room, alone and having her third cup of coffee, when he appeared.

He pulled up a chair beside her. This was such a marked difference from the way he'd been keeping his distance, that she immediately knew he had some suspicions.

"Travis," she said brightly. "How nice to see you up and about. And you look very well, too. I'm so glad you did not suffer much in this last episode."

He looked at her searchingly. He could see no sign of an embarrassed maiden who had been violated. In fact, she seemed remarkably cheerful.

"I understand you relieved Phillips last night, which was very kind of you. Did you get bored? I do not think that is the most stimulating task, sitting with an ailing man."

She smiled at him. She could answer that honestly.

"I was not bored at all. It was such a beautiful night, and I had much to think about."

He looked into her clearly honest eyes, and could see no sign of distress. Still, he worried.

"Elizabeth, I had strange dreams last night. Most of them involved you in a manner that concerns me. They were most realistic and I find I have to ask you what I hope is a ridiculous question. Did I molest you in any way last night?"

Elizabeth breathed an inward sigh. This too, she could answer honestly. Looking at his beloved face, she said simply, "No, Travis, you did not molest me in any manner."

His face cleared, and with a touch of his lips to her hair, he left the room. Elizabeth gazed after him. She knew she'd just given him peace. But how she wished she could have told him how much she loved him. How she would never forget the joy of joining her body with his.

She couldn't disturb him now. She wondered if she would ever have the chance to tell him, when the knowledge would not distress him. For now, though, it was a wonderful secret she must keep.

Chapter Seventeen

IN SPITE OF HIS RELIEF at Elizabeth's words, Travis' mind still gnawed at him. He decided he'd had enough. He didn't seem to know exactly what to think about anything anymore. He would go to one of his clubs and get away from all the women in his household. If he wanted to sit in a chair and brood, he'd do just that!

He thought he had faced up to the fact that he could never have Elizabeth. His dreams last night had showed him how much he still longed for her. Sometimes when he looked into those clear and beautiful eyes, he thought he saw a glimmer of caring for him. This above all mustn't happen. It was time he arranged for her marriage to another man. Weakened by pain, and disgusted with himself, he was not sure he could do it.

He sat alone, lost in thoughts he did not care for, when David Lansdowne found him.

"I have been looking for you, my friend," Kingsley said. He had not seen Travis since taking him home two nights before, and he had daily sent for word of his condition.

Travis came out of his reverie and looked up with a smile.

"David," he said.

"May I join you in a glass of wine?"

Travis laughed briefly. "I think not, but please have whatever you want. I think I overdid the alcohol last night. It does not appeal to me this morning."

David's eyebrows raised slightly. They had been the best of friends for a long time, and each was convinced he would not have survived the war without the other. When Travis was wounded, Phillips and David between them had gotten him off the field. David well knew that drinking too much was not at all usual for Travis.

"If overindulging eased the pain, I'm glad you did," David said grimly. "Heaven knows you need more help than you generally accept."

As was usual, Travis changed the topic. His health was the last topic he wished to explore.

"I'm glad to see you. Did I thank you for helping me home the other night? You must know I appreciated it. But let's not talk about me. I am already blue-deviled, and welcome the chance to have some decent conversation."

Travis summoned a waiter and ordered wine for David, and then sat back and smiled at his friend.

"Truly, David, it cheers me to see you. There is little worse than thinking one's own petty concerns are earthshaking."

Kinsgley snorted. "I have never known anyone less likely to misconstrue the severity of his concerns. Do you care to talk about it?"

Travis sighed. "Not yet, my friend. If any good could come from such a discussion, you would be the one I would turn to. But at present I would rather know about you. How are you enjoying being back in London?"

David gave him a penetrating look and decided he couldn't force the issue. He would talk to Travis on his own terms, at least for a while.

"My mother is happy I'm home, but ringing a peal over my head at not being married at my advanced age. I swear if she suggests another insipid young miss for me to look over I'll not be responsible for even being polite."

Travis grinned. "As I recall it, she's been after you for years to set up your nursery. Don't tell me you can't find anyone in the current crop of society's finest?"

Travis had a good idea where this conversation was heading. He knew David very well indeed, and thought he had sought him out with another purpose than just a health check on his friend.

David gave him a sharp look, and ran his hand through his thick gray hair.

"I see you well recall my mother and her machinations. Her dearest wish is to see grandchildren around her knees. Since my sister Sarah's husband died prematurely, I am the last hope of the Lansdowne's, and she never lets me forget it. However, that doesn't signify. While I honor my lady mother, she does not rule my life. What does signify is that I have found someone who might inspire me to oblige my mother. However, I only say 'might'. I need to know your feelings about Miss Drayton."

David looked at him intently, and Travis steadfastly returned the look. He could find nothing to say at the moment. This was what he had both hoped for, and dreaded.

"To put it bluntly, I've noticed you looking at her at times when she isn't observing you, and I think you have a great deal of feeling for her. If that is so, I would know it."

"Ah," said Travis. "I must be more careful."

"Then I am right. You think of her as much more than your ward."

Travis glanced up at him and rubbed his hands wearily over his eyes.

"I see this is going to be a difficult discussion. Yes, I do think of her as more than my ward, however my guardianship of her is what is critical. Her welfare is dear to me. Personally and from a sense of honor I must put her first at all times. If you've gotten even a hint of how I feel about her, then I've been woefully remiss."

David looked at him, puzzled.

"I don't see that caring for her is being remiss. I think you would be eminently suited. She is exceptional, and I could easily care for her too, but I will not give her another thought. Don't fret for me. I haven't yet lost my heart. It is more a matter of possibility with me. I won't pursue her further."

David got up to leave, placing his hand on his friend's shoulder. Travis gripped it with his own, holding him in place.

"Stay, my friend. You don't understand at all what I am trying to tell you."

"How can I not? If you care for her in the slightest, then I'll remove myself immediately."

Travis rubbed his hand over his face.

"Hear me out, David. Yes, I do care for her. I could care for her even more, but I'll not indulge in such selfishness. I have no certain future. Do you think I could ask Elizabeth, who deserves only the finest, to link herself to a man who could become paralyzed at any time? She would never reproach me, but do you think I want her tied down to an invalid who might never walk again? She must never know me as other than the guardian who did his best for her. Perhaps you are that best."

David looked at him with respect, and hoped the pity he was feeling didn't show.

"But you can offer a woman a good deal. Your wife would be the Countess of Cade, with wealth and an assured place in society."

Travis was not a bit taken in. It was a valiant attempt, but he doubted if David believed it.

"You know society and wealth are not important to me, and I'll wager they are not to Elizabeth. What is important is that I never know when the next attack will occur, or if the bullet fragment will move wrongly, and I am paralyzed. Do you seriously think I'd ask Elizabeth to share such a life?"

"Forgive me if I am prying, but have you consulted the specialists here in London?"

"No one here can offer any suggestion but an operation that none of them has enough faith to tackle. I fear it is something I have to live with, but I'll not ask Elizabeth to share that sort of life."

A silence fell between them, with each man going over what had already been said. Finally David tried yet again.

"I think you are misjudging Elizabeth. I would guess that if she cares for you, she'd want to share with you whatever future you have. I think you should let her make up her own mind. She's not of the ordinary mold."

"Of course she's not, and that is exactly why I can't say anything. She must never know I have any feelings for her beside that of an affectionate guardian. I fear she would sacrifice her future if I asked her. She is as selfless as she is beautiful. You'd be perfect for her, David. I strongly urge you to pursue her."

If David noticed the lines of strain on Travis' face, he did not comment. In fact, he could think of little more to say. He'd heard enough to be convinced that the Earl cared for Elizabeth deeply, but would not permit his emotions to rule him. He would never speak to Elizabeth of the fervent feelings in his heart. But how could he, David, court a woman his best friend loved?

Travis easily sized up his thoughts.

"Have done, David. I would not have her go through life alone. You are the best of men. If I cannot have her, then I'd be pleased to see her happy with you. There is no man I admire more. You can give her all I can, plus a healthy body. If you think you can come to truly care for her, you have my good wishes."

David was too overcome to do anything but to shake his friend's hand, clap him on the shoulder, and leave. His mind was completely unresolved about what he should do. It was the most damnable situation.

David kept to himself for several days. He would not take a chance of harming his friendship with Travis. But suppose David could be the one to make Elizabeth happy, would that not be helping Travis? Wouldn't it be far worse if she settled for an unhappy marriage, and Travis had to endure watching that! His thoughts veered back and forth like a wind-vane. He knew his friend well enough to know he'd never let Elizabeth know of his deep feelings for her.

Elizabeth intrigued David. Her vitality and intelligence captivated him, and then there was her very striking appearance. Memories of her knowledgeable discussion of the pleasures of racing horses, visions of her laughing up at him teasingly, her beautiful smile; all kept her often in his mind. He was half-way in love, and suspected he could fall the rest of the way. His thoughts kept circling, and the outcome was a decision to keep close track of the situation. If Travis seriously urged him on, he would try his hand at securing her. It would be an insult to Travis to do otherwise. In the meantime, he would test the waters a little, and see if her heart were really free. He did not want a bride who cherished another in her heart.

It was early days yet, and he'd carefully observe them both.

Chapter Eighteen

AFTER MUCH CAREFUL thought David decided the usual courting measures would never work with a girl as unusual as Elizabeth. He finally sent round a note inviting her to go with him to see the Elgin marbles. He was right in that she was delighted by the chance to see the sculptures, which the British Museum had recently acquired. But he had not counted on the prettily worded note that accompanied her acceptance. She begged that Claire be allowed to join them. He had hoped for only a maid as a chaperone, who might perhaps be bribed to give him a little privacy. He shrugged and sent another short note saying how pleased he would be to take them both.

The chosen day was a beautiful one, and his horses were eager and restive. Kingsley had to concentrate on getting them settled, while Elizabeth sat quietly, impressed by his skill. He had a reputation of being a wonder with the ribbons, and she enjoyed watching him maneuver the team through the traffic.

Once in the museum, Elizabeth headed straight for the friezes. She had the knack of completely losing herself in any activity she relished, and it was obvious she thought the marbles were exquisite. David watched her enthusiastic face instead of the marbles. Absorbed, neither one of them noticed when Claire wandered into the next gallery.

Her friends were not in sight when Reginald Forbush came round the corner, bowed low, and kissed Claire's gloved hand. He let his lips linger far too long, and she pulled her hand away, trying to repress a shudder.

"This must be my most fortunate day," he said. "I have waited for some time for a chance to talk alone with you."

Claire started, looking frantically around for her companions. She not only disliked Forbush, something about him quite alarmed her, but didn't want to be alone with him even a moment.

Forbush again took her hand, grasping it tightly.

"Do not try to leave, my lady. You and I have much to talk about. It is time for us to become much better acquainted."

Claire recovered her composure enough to look at him with disdain.

"Sir, we have nothing in common, and nothing to discuss. Please let go of my hand."

Forbush smiled in a way that sent ripples of fright through her slender body.

"I would like to hold much more than your hand, my dear. You will soon know what I mean."

His gaze raked her figure, and his lips curled as he seemed to catalogue her every curve.

Claire looked at him in amazement, tinged with the fear now distressing her.

"Sir, would you force me to call for my friends?"

"My beautiful Claire, don't be so hasty. You must accustom yourself to my company, and my caresses. I intend to be your husband, and a very affectionate one at that."

Cringing, Claire could only think he had taken leave of his senses. She tried again to pull away, but he grabbed her arm painfully.

"Be still, my dear. You must learn to pay attention to what I say. As my wife I will demand strict obedience."

Claire was terrified. Still her pride made her gather her courage, and she spoke disdainfully.

"Your wits have gone begging. I will never marry you. Now let me pass."

Forbush let her go a step or two before he said, "You are very wrong, milady. Or do you prefer to have that beloved brother of yours duel with me over the matter?"

Claire stopped short. "Duel with you? Why should Travis duel with you? You are truly mad!"

"Do not deceive yourself. I can easily force him to challenge me."

Claire tossed her head. "Travis is an excellent shot. Even if you could force him, you are a dead man."

"That would only happen if I challenge him. If he challenges me, I get to choose the weapon. I will choose the rapier. No matter his skill, his leg will doom him. He will be completely unable to evade my thrusts. Is his death preferable to marriage to me? I think not."

His sneering words penetrated her fear and loathing. Travis was no longer agile. He would be helpless before Forbush's sword. She wasn't overly familiar with the laws of dueling, but she thought he spoke the truth about who picked the weapon.

Just then David and Elizabeth came through the door. Claire turned to join them, but Forbush grabbed her arm viciously.

"Do not make the error of telling anyone of this conversation. I'll be in touch very soon." He disappeared behind a pillar.

"Claire," said Elizabeth, hurrying over. She was shocked at the girl's stricken appearance. "You have gone quite pale! Is it too warm for you? Would you like to leave?"

Claire made a valiant effort to compose herself.

"I would like some fresh air. But have you seen enough, Eliza? I hate to ruin your afternoon."

She tried frantically to keep her mind on what she was saying, but it was almost hopeless. Should she tell Elizabeth? Would telling anyone put Travis in additional danger? She needed a man to consult on the etiquette of dueling, but she did not know Kingsley well enough.

She let Elizabeth and David usher her from the museum, Elizabeth holding her hand and watching her. As her color returned and reassured her companions, they started home and continued a discussion they had been having about the Marbles.

Elizabeth felt very strongly the Marbles should have been left in Greece.

"I know Lord Elgin thought they might be irreparably damaged by the war, but he had no real right to take them. He took them without the permission of the Greek government! How can you say that is right?"

Kingsley smiled at her indignation. "But you have just thoroughly enjoyed seeing them. How can anything that gives such pleasure be wrong?"

"They are truly beautiful, I'll agree. But seeing them in their own setting must be incomparable. And they are not really ours. Lord Elgin was wrong to take them."

"But then you would likely never have seen them. Think of the pleasure they are bringing so many in London." The gleam in his eyes told her he was trying to keep the argument going.

Elizabeth laughed. "I'm not sure you really think this. Are you bamming me, Lord Kingsley?"

"No, dear lady, I am not. Not much, at least. But I think you are taking a more moral viewpoint than I. Let us start a new discussion. Do you think women are generally more moral than men?"

Elizabeth gestured her hands in the air in mock amazement.

"Lord Kingsley, you are reprehensible! How can I argue that question, when the man I know best, Lord Cade, is the epitome of honor, and I would wager you're the same. Or you could not be his close friend. I suspect you merely enjoy a lively conversation.

Kingsley had to admire her perspicacity.

"Dear lady, you are onto me. I do love an argument with a friend whose intelligence I can admire, as I do yours. Would you prefer that we talk about the latest fashions then?"

The gleam in his eye told Elizabeth he well knew that was not a subject she preferred, so she laughingly switched to the political situation, and the unpopularity of the Prince Regent. They were soon so engrossed in this new topic they did not notice that Claire sat silently in the corner. Amicably bickering, David and Elizabeth kept up their chatter, and Claire slipped away and up the stairs when they reached Cade House.

Chapter Nineteen

CLAIRE SAT IN HER ROOM, her mind in turmoil. She had no doubt Forbush would be able to force Travis to challenge him. All he had to do was make a public statement disparaging his sister's honor, and Travis would be obliged to challenge. Duels were forbidden by law, but they were still the way gentlemen sometimes used to settle an affair of honor. She thought Forbush was correct that the challenged party could pick the weapon. Travis was an excellent swordsman, but his leg could give under him at any time, and he didn't have the agility to evade a murderous charge. That, of course, would not matter to him. He would fight the duel. Nor was it completely certain he would lose, but it was a chance she did not dare take with her beloved brother.

She didn't know where to turn. Elizabeth could not help, nor her mother. She did not dare tell Travis. He would issue the dreaded challenge the moment he heard how she'd been accosted. Pleading a headache, she asked for dinner to be sent to her room, and begged to be excused from going to the theatre.

Both Elizabeth and her mother visited her before they left for the theatre, as Claire seldom had the headache. However, one look at her pale face convinced them that she needed her bed.

"My dear Claire," asked Elizabeth, "can I get you anything? A cool cloth? Did we stay too long at the museum? I must confess I found it such an enjoyable experience that I did not think to check on how you liked it."

Claire shook her head. There was nothing she could explain to Elizabeth. At least not now.

"Don't fret about me, Eliza, I will come about. Perhaps we can go to Hatchard's tomorrow. Travis tells me there is a new shipment of books."

The words were correct, but Elizabeth felt she was missing something important. There was too much anxiety in Claire's expression to be explained by a headache. Puzzled, she changed the subject since she didn't know how to force a confidence.

"May I at least send your abigail to you? I so dislike leaving you alone."

Claire forced a smile.

"Don't worry so, Elizabeth. I will get a good night's sleep, which you must admit is a rarity, and be right as rain. Just enjoy the theatre, and tell me all about it tomorrow."

She burrowed deeper in her bed, and turned her face slightly away, as if she were too tired to talk anymore. Something did not ring true to Elizabeth. She felt Claire's obvious unease was due to more than fatigue, but she could hardly probe when the carriage was waiting.

She dropped a kiss on Claire's forehead and left. Perhaps she could push for a confidence tomorrow.

Claire spent the night relentlessly going over the conversation with Forbush. She couldn't think what to do. Toward dawn, sheer exhaustion took over, and she fell into a fretful slumber.

She couldn't evade the next night's activities. She knew both Elizabeth and her mother were worried, and she felt she had to attend the soiree at Lord and Lady Thorpe's.

Lady Thorpe, of the highest ton, followed her own inclinations and did not subscribe to the general feeling that she must have a huge crowd to have a successful party. It was only to be a small part of a hundred or so families, with dancing for the younger set, and card tables for the older. Besides, she knew her mother and Lady Lavinia, who adored whist, were looking forward to the cards, and she did not want to spoil their pleasure. She was terrified she'd soon have to distress them all.

Travis murmured his regrets for not accompanying them, and for once Claire was grateful to be without him. He was much too adept at sensing her moods.

As the ladies entered the Thorpe townhouse, they saw most of their friends were already there. Lady Lavinia and Lady Rivington immediately started for the card room, leaving Claire and Elizabeth talking with Lord Stokely. Claire was dressed in a white lawn gown that fell softly around her slight figure, but the lack of color emphasized her pallor. She looked as ethereal as an angel.

As they stood talking, they were joined by Forbush. Lord Stokely turned to Claire.

"The dancing is started. May I have the pleasure of the next set?"

Forbush briefly examined his nails and spoke with unusual arrogance.

"But I cannot allow that, my dear sir. She had already promised many of her dances to me. You must wait your turn, if indeed she decides to grant you one."

With a smirk he placed Claire's hand on his arm, and led her to the floor. Flushing deeply, Claire only looked down and allowed him to lead her away.

Lord Stokely looked after them silently. He was far too well bred to reveal his astonishment, but something was not right. It was not like Lady Claire to allow such familiarity, and she'd not seemed pleased. In fact, she'd seemed frightened. He was determined to find out what this was about. He'd not definitely fixed his interest on Lady Claire, but he did not want to see her flummoxed by a cad like Forbush. All London knew he was deep in dun territory, and that he needed a rich wife.

Elizabeth also stood silent. This was so unlike Claire as to be alarming. Claire barely tolerated the man! She'd definitely flinched when he had taken her hand. She looked at them dancing, and saw that Claire never raised her eyes from the floor. Her face had gone from being quite pale, to an unhealthy flush.

Just then Robbie came up.

"Miss Drayton, I hope you have this dance free. And have you seen Claire? I would like to ask her to save me one also."

"You will find her on the floor with Forbush," Stokely said.

Surprised, Robbie looked up and spotted her quickly. Her cheeks were crimson, and she was making no attempt to speak to her partner. Forbush made several attempts at conversation, but she kept her head down and made no answer. Forbush only laughed. At the end of the set, he walked her off the floor, his hands gripping hers as he again placed one on his arm. He stood talking to her, while she made no attempt at polite response.

"This is beyond strange," said Elizabeth. "I cannot like it."

"Nor I," said Robbie grimly. "Let us observe a while. I will take action if I must."

On the other side of the dance floor, Forbush spoke just as grimly to Claire, even as he kept smiling.

"You will dance the next dance after this with me, my girl, and then I will take you into supper. After that I will claim a third dance. The *ton* will know what that means."

Claire was horrified. Only two dances were permissible unless you intended an alliance. A third dance was as good as announcing an engagement. She felt completely helpless. If she left the party, he would likely follow her home and issue the dreaded insult to Travis. What could she do that would not involve Travis in dreadful danger?

Just then Robbie came up to her with a smile.

"Lady Claire, may I have the next dance?" He sketched a bow to Forbush, and then took one of Claire's hands, holding it as tightly as Forbush had. This time, Claire felt the pressure to be warm and welcome, and she relaxed her hand a little in his.

"I know you will excuse us, Forbush. But rest assured I will return Lady Claire to her family after this set. I would not be so rude as to worry her mother."

Forbush flushed at this set down, but relinquished Claire. It was too public a place to risk an altercation. Robbie immediately started with Claire toward the dance floor.

"My dear Lady Claire," he said to the top of her head, "If there is something wrong I beg you to let me assist you."

Claire's terror was such that she could not speak. She lifted her head long enough to flash Robbie an anguished glance. Robbie was completely unmanned as he spotted the tears pooling in her beautiful eyes. If they spilled over it would be a disaster. He bent his head closely over her, and whispered softly, "Listen to me, Claire. I am going to step upon the hem of your gown, and hopefully rip it. If not, you will be so kind as to pretend it is ripped, and tell me you have to go fix it. If you seem upset it will be understandable. Then go to the nearest parlor and wait for me. I will give your excuses to your family, and take you home. You must not stay here any longer. Whatever the problem, I'll take care of it. Will you trust me to see you safely home?"

His understanding, plus the prospect of at least temporary relief, allowed Claire to give him a shaky smile, and continue briefly with the dance. Robbie made an exceptionally clumsy misstep, and indeed tore a big gap near the hem of her skirt. Apologizing profusely, he led her off the floor, and waited in the hall until he saw her slip into a nearby parlor. Going quickly to Elizabeth, he quietly stated that he was taking Claire home to her maid, and would answer for her safety.

"May I go with you?" asked Elizabeth. "I know something is not right with Claire."

"No, you cannot," stated Robbie. "I do not want to alert anyone by interrupting the ladies at whist, which would be necessary if we all leave. Please do not be concerned. I think I have the situation in hand. I will use the family coach to forestall gossip, and then send the coach back for you."

He started to turn away, and then wheeled back.

"You can do one thing, Elizabeth. If Forbush starts after us, try to divert him."

With that he strolled nonchalantly to the side of the room, edging nearer to the hall. Elizabeth stared after him. This was a confident Robbie, who seemed to know exactly what he was doing. It was not the Robbie she knew. Just then she saw that Forbush realized Robbie was alone and leaving, and headed determinedly toward him. Elizabeth cut in front of Robbie to speak to Forbush in such a friendly manner that he could do nothing but stop and speak with her. Robbie slipped silently out of the room.

He swiftly went to the parlor, carrying Claire's white velvet pelisse, carefully wrapped her in it, and escorted her to carriage. He kept up a line of constant recrimination about his clumsiness, and how he hoped her maid could repair the damage. He bundled her into the carriage, and told the driver Lady Claire needed to return to Cade House. He then turned his anxious attention to Claire.

Claire huddled in one corner of the coach, sobbing softly. The relief of escaping Forbush let loose her tears. She had no idea of how to escape the beast but she somehow trusted Robbie to help. At least she wasn't forced to endure his hated presence, not with Robbie beside her.

Robbie looked at the sobbing girl, her fair head bowed over her hands. With a muttered and very unclerical curse, he moved next to her and drew her into his arms. After all, he told himself, if he had a sister in such distress he hoped someone would do the same. But Claire melted against him, and buried her face in his coat. The slight yet definite curves of her body, and the delightful feel of her in his arms made him realize he wasn't feeling a bit brotherly.

He'd known for some time that his love for Elizabeth was not only hopeless, but changing. He would always cherish her, but he'd come to realize they were intellectually inclined in different directions. Essentially they would not suit. He did not want to be a cat's paw to a brilliant wife. Now he was aware of the faint lavender perfume from Claire's hair, her lissome body, and the fact that she was clinging to him in a most delightful fashion. He smiled to himself wryly. Claire was after all, sister to a powerful and wealthy Earl. While he himself was well born, he did not want to be branded as a fortune hunter. Why couldn't he manage to be attracted to a female he could more easily pursue? Enough of that, he told himself, it was time to help the girl in his arms.

He set her a little away from him, and patted her tears dry with his handkerchief.

"Come, my dear. You must tell me what has so overcome you. I am well used to confessions, you know, and yours can't be so bad. I'm sure it had to do with Forbush, who is not worth one of your tears."

Fresh tears welled up in Claire's eyes at the hated name, but she struggled to speak. "You have been so kind. I do truly thank you. I'm not often such a watering pot."

The wavering smile undid him again, and he drew her to him, but loosely, this time. "Of course you're not," he said. She seemed content to rest in his embrace, but he urged her to speak. "I can't solve the problem until I know what it is," he said simply. "Believe me, a clergyman hears many strange stories. You cannot shock me, you know. And almost anything can be fixed, if you go about it properly."

Claire stiffened. "I have done nothing that will shock you, Mr. Carstairs. But perhaps the wickedness of that horrid man will."

Robbie smiled grimly to himself. She was going to tell him. He forced the responses of his very interested body to the back of his mind, and concentrated on listening intently. Now was not the time to dwell on the fact that she was a beautiful girl he'd like very much to kiss. Even more to the point, she was turning to him to help her, as Elizabeth had never done. She was looking at him with confidence and trust, and he had seldom felt so pleased. It was enough for now.

"I am terribly afraid. You see," she paused for a great gulp of air. "I must marry him. And I can hardly bear his touch!"

Robbie stared at her. He had not expected this!

"My dear girl, that is ridiculous! Why on earth would you think such a thing? I'm sure you've done nothing to give him such a presumptuous idea."

He looked down at the girl curled against him, and was completely baffled. She was so obviously an innocent.

"You had best tell me all of it," he stated.

With a heartfelt sigh of relief, Claire poured out the whole story. How she knew that Forbush only wanted her marriage settlement, but he planned to force Travis to a duel if she did not agree. Travis' health would likely mean that he would lose the duel. She would have to marry a man she hated.

Robbie's first reaction was one of relief. This was the act of a desperate cad, and one that could easily be addressed. He'd been afraid of something much more serious, but knowing how unworldly Claire was, he could see how this seemed catastrophic to her. To be sure, Travis could not be allowed to fight a duel unless he chose the weapons, but Robbie thought he could deal with that.

He lightly kissed the top of her head.

"My dear, this is something I can manage. I may be a clergyman, but I am a man first of all. No one in my care shall come to harm. Will you let me deal with this as I see fit?"

"Oh, if you only would! But how can you? A clergyman cannot fight a duel! How will you deal with this monster?"

Robbie smiled down at her.

"I certainly cannot fight a duel that could result in death. But there are other ways besides killing to fight, and I am adept at several. Your brother is in no danger, nor are you. Will you trust me to help you?"

Claire looked at him with adoration in her eyes. It was all Robbie could do to keep from holding her tighter and kissing her, but he felt she'd endured enough turmoil for one evening. He would prove himself to her first, and then God willing, think about what these new feelings entailed. He realized he was not the most eligible man for a match with Lady Claire Rivington. However, his birth was impeccable, and perhaps she did not care overmuch about material advantages. Right now there was this little matter of squelching an obnoxious worm. And that would be a pleasure!

Lost in his thoughts, he became aware that the girl he was holding loosely in his arms had grown limp. Looking down, he saw that she had fallen asleep, as trusting as a child. He shifted her so that she would be more comfortable, and let her doze. He would take care of her. His chosen profession, which perfectly suited his protective character, would assure that in any case. Since he was more than casually interested in the girl he was cradling, his shielding her was guaranteed.

When they reached Cade House, Robbie gently wakened her, and helped her from the carriage to the door where the butler was waiting.

"Please call Lady Claire's maid," he said. "She is very tired, and should go immediately to bed, with no disturbance from any one."

Jamieson nodded and assisted the sleepy Claire into the house. Seeing that she was safe and taken care of, Robbie left. Now he had only to finalize the plan that was forming in his head. He found he was looking forward with delight to settling accounts with Reginald Forbush. It might not be clerically admirable but he had conceived a vast disgust of the man. He would be honored to disgrace him in the eyes of the *ton,* and in doing so he would free Claire forever from his machinations.

Accordingly, he went to White's. It was time for the first move.

Chapter Twenty

ROBBIE WALKED THROUGH the rooms of White's, stopping occasionally to speak to one of his friends. He did not allow himself to get caught up in a conversation however, as he was intent on finding Forbush. In fact, he was prepared to spend the evening going the round of clubs until he found him.

After about an hour at White's he went across the street to Brooks. He found Forbush there, seated at a table of *vingt-et-un*, gambling recklessly, and from the scowl on his face, losing. Robbie went immediately to take up a stand behind his chair. Forbush had evidently been drinking heavily. His face was flushed and his appearance disheveled, his cravat slightly rumpled. He fingered his cards, showing little of the *savoir-faire* that was essential to a winning player. This was exactly the way Robbie had hoped to find him.

Robbie stood motionless behind him for some ten minutes, and several times Forbush turned around and glared at him. Finally Robbie sauntered around the table until he was facing Forbush. Staring directly into his eyes, Robbie casually adjusted the lace at his cuffs, and then turned to Roger Stanton, who was also at the table.

"In faith, Sir Stanton," Robbie drawled, "I wonder why you play with a person who does not abide by a gentleman's rules of the game."

He spoke in such a bored tone that it took a moment for the meaning to penetrate. Sir Stanton looked quickly at Forbush, who was slowly taking in the fact that he had just been publicly insulted. And with an insult that not even a prompt apology could allay. Forbush suddenly pushed back his chair.

"I say, Carstairs, if you are implying anything, come out with it!"

"After watching your method of play, Forbush, I merely stated what I saw. I would not deign to play with you, and I am surprised you find many who do."

There was a collective silence. No one, but no one, could let such a statement pass. Forbush lunged at Robbie, who neatly sidestepped him and caught him by his right arm, which he then twisted behind his back.

"Pray let us not have a public brawl. If you choose to challenge me, do so, but let's be gentlemen and settle our differences outside the club."

Livid with rage, Forbush shouted. "Of course I challenge you, you religious idiot. Name your seconds and your weapons. Or will you claim the privilege of being a man of God to escape your just desserts?"

With a barely discernable smile, Robbie let go of his arm and stepped away. Seeing that Lord Stokely had come during the uproar, he quickly asked him and Sir Stanton to second him, and both accepted with hints of smiles. Robbie's own smile of satisfaction was now more obvious. He turned to Forbush.

"It's true I am a man of the Church, and so I must disdain any weapon that might kill a man. My religion does not, however, keep me from administering justice. I have two weapons with which I'm adept, and I choose the first one. A horsewhip."

At the excited murmur, and seeing the stunned look on Forbush's face, he added calmly, "Perhaps a horsewhip frightens you. No one will call you a coward for that. If you wish I offer you my second choice, which is fisticuffs. In either case, while I will not kill you, I will most certainly mark you."

Forbush seemed unable to respond. Robbie waited a moment, and then added, "I would suggest three mornings from now at six o'clock. I would like time to practice my skill with the whip. Our seconds can fix the details. But if whips are too frightening, say so at once, and we will go to the alternative."

Forbush turned and left the room. He could not choose fisticuffs without branding himself a coward. Somehow that sanctimonious young cur had managed to force him into a fight with whips! He shuddered at the thought of the pain and disfigurement that could ensue. This was not at all the type of duel he wanted, nor even the person he wanted to engage. In truth, he'd never seriously thought his actions would force a duel with anyone, but hoped to frighten Claire into his hands.

After Robbie and his seconds left, laughing and with arms linked together, the room erupted. Duels were technically illegal, but were still a favorite way of settling an affair of honor. But no one had ever heard of using horsewhips. Carstairs must be indeed confident of his skill to suggest such a weapon. Some in the room knew that Carstairs had long been one of Gentleman Jackson's favorite pupils and one of the few he deigned to spar with personally. If fisticuffs was his second choice, how skilled he must be using a whip.

Since duels were legally forbidden, talk about them was generally circumspect and confined to the clubs. Certainly it was very bad form to mention it to any of the women in your life. Would a duel with whips, where no likely death was involved, even be illegal?

This was too delicious a subject to be ignored. Soon most of the masculine members of the *ton* knew that Carstairs had deliberately provoked a challenge from Forbush, and the gossips speculated as to why a young man of Carstair's profession would knowingly do such a thing. To be sure, he'd seen to it that he would not likely kill his man. But with his connections, he could expect to go far in the church, and this might make a mull of his future.

Why then, had he done it? Assuredly not because he caught Forbush cheating, even if it seemed obvious he had. That was a charge few cared to make, since proof was so difficult, especially when the accuser was not one of the players. Could there be a woman involved? After all, Carstairs was young and handsome. But who was she?

The whole affair rapidly became the most interesting scandal broth of the season. Bets were made in the book at White's as to not only who would win, would they actually use whips, and even if the duel would take place at all. Rumor soon escalated that Robbie and his brothers had practiced with whips when young, seeing who could most quickly dislodge red flannel scraps from the top of a wall. Rumor also said Robbie usually won.

If Carstairs were really that adept, most felt they would not care to meet him with a horsewhip in his hand. Rumors then circulated about Robbie's ability with his fists, but everyone agreed Forbush could not now honorably pick that second choice. The general and delicious consensus was that Forbush would be dealt with in a most painful manner. Men looked at Carstairs with new and appreciative eyes, all of them deciding they would not want to be Forbush.

At the soiree, Elizabeth had dealt with the situation Robbie had left her with, casually chatting with friends, and then going to find the older ladies at their whist.

"Claire has gone home with a slight headache, and I am ready to go or stay at your command. Are you having a good game?"

Lady Rivington looked worried for a moment, and then seeing how relaxed Elizabeth appeared, decided not to fret.

"I am afraid I am not the best of players, even though I love the game. Lavinia is doing very well. But don't you want to dance more, child? You are in such looks, and I saw how would-be-swains flocked to you the moment you entered."

Elizabeth had to laugh at this exaggeration.

"You flatter me unduly, ma'am. And I'm quite content to either go or stay, as I had said. I fear I am a creature most easily pleased."

Lady Rivington patted her hand. "You are a courteous young lady, and I think I *would* like to leave soon. I find I do better if I do not have too many late nights. 'Tis a far cry from when I was your age and danced the night away!"

"Then you are better than I ever was," said Elizabeth. "I have never yet danced 'til dawn."

She watched the end of the game, and then gathered the ladies and their wraps and started casually toward the hall, stopping to talk to friends along the way.

Since the carriage had returned and was waiting for them, they soon all returned to Cade House, Elizabeth chattering the whole way. As soon as she could, she stole down the hall to Claire's room, only to find her sound asleep, a peaceful smile on her face. Puzzled, she crept away. At least Claire had resolved some part of her problem and was safe for the night. Now she'd learn nothing till morning.

Fortunately for Elizabeth's curiosity, the next morning found Claire eagerly coming to her room and confiding the whole story. Thrilled at the masterful way Robbie had taken over her problems, Claire was anxious to tell someone who could understand how exceptional he was.

It also found Travis going to his club and hearing rumors that baffled him. All he could gather for certain was that Carstairs had issued a challenge that had everyone buzzing with excitement. No one seemed to know why, except that they all agreed a beautiful woman was involved.

His immediate reaction was a burst of sheer murderous temper that Carstairs would involve himself in any way with protecting Elizabeth. Of course it was Elizabeth, as the woman Robbie had long pursued. Carstairs had no such right. Protecting her was the prerogative of Travis, and his alone!

A few moments reflection convinced him he had better make sure of his facts before storming out of the house and accosting Carstairs. He thought Elizabeth the most likely explanation, but he had better make certain. It would not do to accuse Carstairs unjustly.

Accordingly, he set out to find Carstairs, and find him he did, sitting silently by the big bay window at White's. A glass of sherry was in his hands, and a deeply contemplative look on his face. Travis stood looking at him for a moment, and then quietly went up and asked if he could join him.

"Of course, my lord, do sit down. Will you have a glass of sherry or do you prefer something stronger?"

"Sherry suits my mood admirably," answered Travis. "But if the rumors are true, I wonder that you are sitting here so peaceably, with such a mild drink. Most men who have just issued a challenge to a duel would resort to something stronger."

Robbie looked up at him calmly.

"I do not need drink to bolster my courage, nor do I see much reason to be afraid. I assure you I know exactly what I am doing."

Travis looked at him with admiration. A horsewhip could be a terrible weapon, cutting a man to pieces, or flaying him alive. That this was the weapon of Robbie's choice said a great deal about his courage and daring. Travis thought he would have loved to have had young Carstairs under his command in the war. He'd be exceptional in any profession. As a third son the church had been one of his few choices, but Travis thought the church was lucky to have him. Courage combined with sweetness of character was unusual.

They sat sipping their sherries. Robbie wondered just how much Travis knew. He would answer any question honestly, but as briefly as possible.

Travis finally spoke. "I do not know how to lead into this, so will ask you straightly. Is my ward in any way the cause of your forcing a duel on Forbush?"

"No, she is not," said Robbie flatly.

Travis could not help a small sigh. "Then you have not only reassured me beyond measure, but have taken all the wind from my sails. I was determined that if Elizabeth were involved, then you yield your place in the duel to me. She is most definitely my responsibility, and my pleasure to protect."

Robbie looked at him gravely, and hid his secret delight that Travis had asked a question he could answer honestly. Travis must never guess it was Claire's honor he was fighting for. All would be lost if Travis suspected that Claire had gotten herself into such a coil by trying to protect her brother from protecting her. Moreover, he thought the Earl's seeking him out to be revealing. He had long suspected that the Earl had a *tendre* for his ward that he carefully concealed.

"I assure you that Miss Drayton is in no way involved. As a gentleman you know I cannot discuss particulars with you. Suffice it to say your ward is not the cause."

Travis could not doubt him.

"I understand Stokely and Stanton are your seconds. Allow me to say that if one of them becomes indisposed, I would be honored to take his place."

Robbie nodded his thanks, but said nothing more.

Having said everything he had come to say, Travis sat for a while longer, asking about Robbie's mother and being assured she was well on the mend.

"I think my presence in town has been essential. While she approves of my vocation, or says she does, she regrets it keeps me from the pleasures of society. She is hopeful every time she summons me to London that I'll find another daughter for her. My two brothers are married, and she will not rest easy until I, too, am leg-shackled."

Travis laughed.

"Mothers are generally agreed that their bachelor sons should marry. I imagine my lady mother and yours have much in common. I am sorely afraid, however, that mine is doomed to disappointment. Yours will be luckier."

With a bow and a handshake, Travis left Robbie staring after him. What an appalling shame it would be if a fine man like Travis meant never to marry. Since he was wealthy, titled, and handsome, it had to be his own decision, and Robbie could not help but wonder why. Most of all, he feared for Elizabeth if Travis stood by his resolve.

He suspected it would shatter her.

The clubs of Brook's and White's buzzed with gossip of the duel, but Elizabeth and Claire had no knowledge of it. They had both cancelled that day's activities to give Claire some relief from the constant social strain. Elizabeth longed for Claire's confidence as to what was bothering her, and was delighted when Claire poured out the whole story. Claire was completely convinced that Robbie would take care of everything. Elizabeth was alarmed by the story, but kept her fears to herself. She could not help but be pleased with Claire's trust in Robbie. They could do little but wait till they heard from him, meanwhile speculating as to what action he might take.

They were mistakenly complacent. Talk raged through the clubs, with the betting getting heavier by the day. Most of the gossip was not shared with the women in the members' lives, as dueling was regarded as strictly a masculine matter. The members were unusually interested in this most peculiar of duels, and did not want any talk to get to a magistrate who might try to stop it.

The only word Claire and Elizabeth received was a note from Robbie to Claire. He begged her pardon for not being able to call for a few days, and asked that she be unusually careful to be surrounded by family and friends if she attended any function outside her home. He told her he'd see her soon, and until then, to be guarded at all times.

He did not want to unduly frighten her, but thought Forbush capable of any trick to solve his desperate situation, and greatly feared he would try to abduct Lady Claire. With her in his hands he could force matters his own way.

Claire immediately saw the sense of his proposal since it mirrored her own thoughts, and resolved to stay in Cade House till she heard from Robbie. She was well content to leave everything in his hands. She was actually delighted to have some time to herself, and away from the social whirl.

They had all been engaged to see Macbeth the next evening. Claire pleaded the need of another night of rest. Travis deputized David to go in his stead, and so Elizabeth and the two older ladies were all escorted by David, and attended the performance at Drury Lane.

The theater was ablaze with lights, and to Elizabeth's eyes it was magnificent, with its double staircase leading to the rotunda. The Cade box was naturally one of the best in the house, and Elizabeth settled happily into one of the velvet seats.

At the first intermission they were joined by Stokely and Stanton. Stanton's formal evening wear was not the regulation black, but a deep maroon that he had offset with pink breeches and a pink satin vest. The ladies tried to keep their fascination from showing, but they didn't quite succeed. Stanton preened under their hasty glances, and Stokely looked on in amusement.

Elizabeth was thrilled by the play, the setting, and the actors. The theatre and the opera were almost enough to make her forswear the countryside she loved. She bubbled over at the gentlemen in the box.

"Is it not one of the most exciting plays ever? I have heard Sarah Siddons played the part or Lady Macbeth so superbly that no one could match her, but I thought this actress was excellent!"

Her endearing enthusiasm made the rather jaded gentlemen smile. It was only one of her many charms, in David's eyes.

"But Lady Claire is not with you," said Sir Stanton. "I trust she is not ill."

"No, not at all," said her mother. "She simply felt the need of an early night. I hope she'll not be distressed when we tell her what a wonderful performance she missed."

"Then we must put together a theater party and make sure Lady Claire attends," commented Lord Stokely. "Such a beautiful and sweet young lady deserves every pleasure life has to offer."

This florid speech rather startled Elizabeth, particularly since Lord Stokely sounded sincere. Evidently Claire had made more than one conquest in this, her first season. David returned to the box just then, and the men chatted, making no mention of the gossip raging in the clubs about Carstairs and Forbush.

IN SPITE OF ALL THE gossip, the proposed affair did not reach the ears of any authorities, and there was no attempt to stop the duel. On the appointed morning, Robbie and his seconds repaired to Hyde Park, and stood waiting for the dawn to break. The pre-dawn skies were barely gray, with a light fog that seemed to be dissipating as they watched. Soon, through the leafy branches, bright colors of red, pink, and orange appeared. More than one assembled thought it was a morning that would make the staunchest hero hope to see another one.

Robbie, however, seemed oblivious of anything but sheer boredom, leaning casually against a tree. Two wickedly thick whips lay coiled on the ground so that Forbush could make his choice. They were ones Robbie and his brothers had used, and were as like as two peas. The doctor was also waiting. He privately thought he could do little for injuries inflicted by a horsewhip. And although Robbie did not know it, the Earl of Cade was sitting quietly in his carriage that was half hidden under the trees. Everyone waited in a preternatural silence.

Six o'clock arrived. Then six-thirty. Still no sound of horse's hooves or a carriage.

Stokely approached Robbie and suggested that they leave the field, since honor had been satisfied and his opponent had not appeared.

Robbie shook his head. "I would give him extra leeway. In such a matter, I would rather wait a few more minutes than condemn a man to the life of a coward."

At six forty-five Robbie's second strode over, declared there would be no duel, and that the honors were to Carstairs. Everyone solemnly shook Robbie's hand, and he accepted each congratulation without smiling. He heaved himself off the tree he had been leaning against and silently headed toward his horse. He had just ruined a man. He did not feel jubilant, even though the man deserved it. There was almost dead quiet in the park. One man whispered he was not surprised at Forbush's choice not to face a horsewhipping.

"I say," Stanton said to Stokely, "what will happen to Forbush now? He's utterly ruined in London!"

"I cannot say that many will care what happens to him," murmured Stokely. "He has put himself beyond the pale. I wouldn't want to be in his shoes."

Stokely gazed after Robbie as he walked away. This was a man he had obviously misjudged, and one he'd like as his friend. Probably Forbush would soon set sail for France, where the disgrace might not follow him. He certainly couldn't remain in London.

These were exactly Robbie's thoughts, and therefore Claire was safe from persecution. Robbie had never thought Travis would permit a marriage to such a scoundrel. She was safe! His only remaining wish was that Travis would never find out the true cause of the duel.

He had better see Claire as soon as possible to reassure her, and also to bind her to secrecy. He would send round a note immediately asking her to drive with him in the afternoon. The morning had ended the way he wanted, but it was hard to feel jubilant at any man's disgrace.

Chapter Twenty-One

ROBBIE STOOD IN THE hallway at Cade House, watching Claire skip down the stairs. She looked adorable and yet elegant, dressed in a deep shade of blue that highlighted her fairness. He thought that one of the most endearing things about her was that she didn't seem to have the faintest idea of her loveliness.

As he handed her into his curricle, she smiled warmly at him.

"Mr. Carstairs, how very prompt you are! I had not even begun to wonder where you were!"

She was very conscious of the listening servants, and did not intend to question him until they were well out of the house.

"Lady Claire, that is a delightful greeting. You must be careful, though. I might be deliberately late next time, in hopes that you would show concern at my delay. That would be a compliment I would treasure."

Claire blushed deeply, and Robbie cursed himself. He kept forgetting what a true innocent she was, and that she was not comfortable with what she thought was society's insincerity.

"My dear Lady Claire," he said warmly, "I did not mean anything except that you look perfectly charming, and you conduct yourself in the same way. You can't know how refreshing you are. But enough of personal talk, which interests me mightily, but I am afraid is difficult for you."

He paused as he directed the horses past a spot crowded with other carriages and dray carts.

Claire watched his skill with appreciation. She felt relaxed, certain somehow he had solved the problem. She fervently hoped he would tell her how he'd gone about it. Her maid had gossiped with the Branleigh twin's maid, who had some outlandish tale of an aborted duel with horsewhips, but she did not credit such an improbable story. She was anxious, however, to hear what had really happened.

Robbie looked at her, and could see no obvious signs of distress. He smiled warmly down at her.

"Will you permit me to neglect you somewhat while I concentrate on getting these fractious horses into the park? Then I assure you I will give you my undivided attention."

As they entered the park, they found it crowded with the usual throng, and were soon surrounded by well-wishers stopping them with polite greetings and curious glances. Obviously something important had happened in the eyes of the fashionable world. Stokely came up to them the minute he spotted them, and stopped his horse. He dismounted and came over to kiss Claire's hand and bow deeply to Robbie.

"Well met, Lady Claire, and Mr. Carstairs. I sincerely wish to pay my respects on the recent affair that was so valiantly managed. All London is filled with admiration for your bravery, Carstairs. I make you my compliments."

Robbie stiffed in dismay, but returned the bow. "As you well know, I was not called upon to exhibit any bravery. The affair is best forgotten."

Stokely laughed.

"Indeed, sir, you are wrong in both cases. You showed uncommon bravery and it will not be forgotten, at least for a fortnight! You must resign yourself to be no less than at least a seven day's hero!"

Claire looked at him with wide-eyed absorption. It soon became apparent that he'd made a very poor choice in coming to the park. He'd thought the affair over and done with, except for his explanation to Claire.

More than one carriage tried to stop them, but he politely waved and went on. Finally he spotted David Lansdowne and Elizabeth, and decided it would be much better to stop and speak with friends than to let Claire meet with any more loose talk.

David and Elizabeth were smiling as they stopped their curricle. Evidently they both knew some version of the story he had hoped to tell Claire privately, and perhaps it was better to tell it before friends.

The two carriages drew close together, and Robbie greeted them with a rather rueful grin. He leaned over and took Elizabeth's hand and kissed it. As he did, he felt as though he were bidding her farewell, as indeed he'd already said goodbye to any image of her in his future. Her eyes widened perceptibly, and he wondered fleetingly if her damnable intelligence deciphered his feelings.

"Well, my friends," Robbie said, "do you intend to be polite, or are you going to ask me what you really want to know? I am not adverse to pound dealing. I've been trying to find a way to tell Lady Claire what happened today, but we've been surrounded ever since we left Cade House."

Kingsley grinned at this frank manner of speaking. "I have told Miss Drayton only that you frightened Forbush out of the country. This seemed to please her enormously. If you wish to elaborate, I for one would dearly love to hear you."

Claire's astonished face made Robbie turn to her.

"Do not fret, my lady. I told you I'd take care of the problem. Let me assure you, it has been taken care of."

"I can get nothing out of this wretch I am with except that you were brave and clever," said Elizabeth. "Can you tell us more, Robbie? We're all hoping for enlightenment."

Robbie decided he could trust Kingsley. He already knew he could trust Elizabeth, of course, and he really needed to tell Claire what had happened.

"If I tell you I beg it will go no further. I took Forbush's rather crude manners and turned them back on him. He'd wanted to provoke a challenge to a duel so he could choose the weapons and have an unfair advantage. I therefore provoked him to challenge me, and the weapons I chose were unpalatable to him. I think we will find he has left the country."

"Oh, Robbie," said Claire softly. Since this was the first time she had used his given name, he cast her a pleased look that didn't escape the two in the other carriage.

Kingsley looked at him in bemusement. "I have a feeling that is all the information we are going to get, Miss Elizabeth," he said.

"You have the gist of the matter," said Robbie. "It does not do to elaborate on another's disgrace. But I cannot keep these cattle standing about. I'd be a wretch to return them to my father in poor condition. I trust you with the information I've given you, as I do not want anyone's name involved in this matter except my own."

Elizabeth laughed. "Don't think you can escape me so easily, Robbie. You've told us very little. There is more to this story than this meager scrap. I warn you, I will have it out of you at some future date."

"With all due respect, Elizabeth, that is all I have to say. I do not intend to elaborate beyond these simple facts, even for you."

He smiled so sweetly that she couldn't take offense at his words. This was a different Robbie than the one she thought she knew.

Elizabeth and David drove on, with Elizabeth speculating on this new Robbie. She wondered if she could get more information out of David.

"Can you tell me anymore than this scrap we have just gotten from my close-mouthed friend? I would dearly love to know what's going on. Robbie is certainly not the type to recklessly provoke a duel. He would never put himself in a position where he would have to kill an opponent. Please, David, I know you can enlighten me."

Kingsley looked at her thoughtfully.

"I can only tell you what I think happened. Forbush challenged Carstairs. I suspect from our meeting today that it had something to do with Lady Claire."

He shot her a questioning look but she did not respond.

"Ah, now *you're* not being forthcoming! In any case, Carstairs picked horsewhips as his weapon of choice. This of course was unprecedented, and caused great interest. Rumor has it that Carstairs and his brothers made a game of practicing with whips when they were younger, that they pretended to be fearless coachmen of the Royal Mail stagecoaches and learned to be quite proficient with whips. As you might have heard, some coachmen could reputedly snare a rabbit with their whip as they sped along, and take it home for dinner. I don't know how close the brothers came to that, but Carstairs is doubtless formidable. Forbush never appeared for the duel."

"Thank God," said Elizabeth.

"Should I make a guess as to the cause of Carstair's provocation?" asked David.

"No, please don't. At all costs I want any mention of this kept from Travis. While I will not admit to anything you are thinking, I know you'll agree Travis must not get the smallest hint. His pride would be seriously affronted."

David did not comment that she had just confirmed his suspicions that Claire was the woman involved.

"Carstairs behaved admirably. We cannot fault him."

"Indeed he did," agreed Elizabeth. She wondered where this affinity between Robbie and Claire was headed. Travis was not excessively high in the instep, but he might want much more for Claire than a country vicar.

Elizabeth and Kingsley continued their ride through the park. Kingsley was an utterly charming companion, and when he returned her to Cade House and handed her out of the carriage, she was laughing and animated. David bowed low over her hand and kissed it.

Travis, standing in the big bow window of the parlor, turned away from the sight.

He returned to his big leather chair, an open volume of Pliny on his knees. He congratulated himself on how well his plans were going. Richard was doing well in school, and Elizabeth was blossoming into the beautiful and charming woman he'd known she was destined to become. A wonderful man was courting her. His sister seemed to be taking a certain amount of enjoyment in the season, and certainly Elizabeth had helped a good deal with that.

Why then was he so dissatisfied and unhappy?

He called for his walking cane and left the house. He found that if he paced himself carefully, walking gave him both exercise and space to think. He prayed that a future attack wouldn't shut off even this slight activity.

RUNNING UP THE STAIRS, Elizabeth went looking for Claire, and found her in her room with the Branleigh twins.

Amelia preened herself as she tried on one of Claire's lately purchased hats.

"If you change your mind about this one, Claire," Amelia coaxed, "I would have you think of me. This is absolutely perfect on me, isn't it Missy?"

The hat was of dark blue velvet, with white satin roses on one side, and tied with a white satin bow. It accented Amelia's auburn hair charmingly, and with her innate good manners Claire immediately offered it to her friend.

"You must take it, Amelia. I have not worn it, so it cannot be termed a castoff."

Amelia backed down in consternation.

"But I cannot take your new hat, my dear Claire. I was only funning, and admiring your excellent taste. Mama would be furious with me if she thought I'd even hinted at such a thing."

"But she need never know. I am perfectly serious in offering it to you. It really does look just the thing on you."

Melissa laughed. "Do take it, Amelia. Claire really wants you to have it. As for me, I think I will cease trying on any of Claire's wardrobe. If we both showed up with purloined items it would be too hard to explain. But you must have found a new milliner, Claire!"

"Are you sure you want to give this delicious hat away? I'm sure it looks equally well on you, and will help you easily find a husband this first season."

"I'm not at all sure I want to," muttered Claire.

"Claire, now you are the one who is funning. Why else does one have a season? I intend to find a husband. I might have already found him," Amelia added.

She took off the hat and turned triumphantly to face her expectant friends.

"I have reason to hope Lord Willoughby will come up to scratch very soon."

There was not the immediate and envious reaction Amelia had expected. In fact there was silence. Lord Willoughby was a Viscount who would soon be an Earl, since his elderly father was most unwell. Lord Willoughby, however, was two inches shorter than Amelia, thirty years older, and definitely paunchy. He had been married before, to a pale little woman who'd given him two sons, and then quietly died. He'd always been very much in the petticoat line, and was notorious for his string of mistresses, even during his marriage. At least one of them had later complained publicly about his cruel streak.

Missy looked embarrassed, but not astonished, She said nothing. Claire recovered first.

"My dear Amelia, if this is what you want, we will all wish you happy. I've noticed you with him, but not excessively. I thought you liked Mr. Carstairs or Lord Stokely."

Amelia tossed her pretty head.

"Of course I do, you clunch. Mr. Carstairs is a handsome hunk to dream about but not to marry. And Lord Stokely's title does not approach Lord Willoughby's future one." She shrugged her shoulders. "Men like Carstairs and

Stokely can wait until I have been wed a year, and then we will see. I intend to be very discreet, but I am sure I can manage Willoughby."

Claire and Elizabeth looked askance at each other, but quickly averted their shocked eyes. This was, after all, the way of the *ton*. Once married, if a wife were discreet, almost any alliance was overlooked. They'd not thought it of Amelia, however.

Missy, now definitely embarrassed, turned to Claire. "And I think you yourself are partial to Lord Stokely and Mr. Carstairs. Would your brother countenance either one as a suitor?"

Claire spoke stiffly. "I do not know what Travis would say, and since neither one are suitors it doesn't matter. However, when the time comes, he's promised I'll have a say in the matter. But do let's change the topic. I find it useless to make idle suppositions."

Seeing that Claire was truly upset, Elizabeth suggested they all go shopping, but the twins had another call to make. After they had left, Elizabeth looked curiously at Claire.

"Why did you get so bothered, my dear Claire? Travis will never insist on a marriage that you do not desire."

Claire shrugged her pretty shoulders and looked away.

"I will not marry without love. And this season is beginning to bore me. It's all so fruitless. Don't you think you'd get bored going to party after party through the years?"

This was more than normal ennui. Elizabeth answered lightly, but with a sincerity Claire could not mistake.

"Of course I do, my love. But what I think doesn't really matter. You know I will go back to my farm after this season, and raise Richard to be the man our father wanted him to be. This present is for me just a delightful interlude. If you want more direction in your future, I'm sure you'll find it. You have too many gifts to squander them on idleness."

Claire heard only that Elizabeth might not always be with her.

"Oh, that cannot be," she wailed. "Losing you! I will not have it!"

Elizabeth, touched to the heart, gave the girl a quick hug.

"Come, let's not worry about things we can't change. We'll be friends no matter where the future takes us. I have just started Miss Austin's new book,

Sense and Sensibility, and I'll finish it quickly so you can have it. You'll love it, I'm sure."

Before she could say anymore, Jamieson appeared with his usually solemn face.

"The Earl requests that Miss Claire join him in the library as soon as possible. You had better hurry, my lady. He seems very stern."

Claire looked at Elizabeth with alarm. "Travis is never stern with me. I'm much afraid he had heard about Robbie and the duel."

Elizabeth smiled slightly. "You goose, you must have known he would!"

"But what shall I tell him?"

"You have no choice but to tell him the truth, if that is what this is about. However, do try to spare his pride if you can. He might take it hard that you turned to another, instead of letting him fight his own battles."

"But right now he cannot!"

Now it was Elizabeth who looked alarmed.

"Believe me, Claire, it will devastate him if he finds you think that. I repeat, you *must* be careful of his pride."

A subdued and worried Claire knocked at the door of the library. She'd never meant to hurt Travis. She'd not given a thought to his considerable pride. She hoped he wasn't truly angry. He had sometimes been disappointed in her, but never truly angry.

She found him seated at this desk, his hands folded in front of him. The look he leveled on her was one of barely concealed annoyance.

"I do not think I have to tell you why I've asked you to come to me. I have heard enough about the duel between Carstairs and Forbush to know you were intimately involved, which I must say I had not suspected. Would you care to tell me about it?"

His tone was perfectly calm, but Claire had no doubt he was keeping a firm rein on his temper.

She lifted her chin bravely. "Yes, I can tell you all about it, and it all resounds to the credit of Mr. Carstairs."

His face softened slightly. "Then do tell me, Claire. I have been piecing together a gaggle of rumors that do not do credit to anyone. Why was Carstairs even involved?"

"He happened upon me at the Thorpe's when I was distraught by the unwelcome attentions of Forbush. I still shudder at the memory of that man, and at the time I was in tears. Mr. Carstairs saw me home safely and volunteered to take care of the matter. I was happy with his offer. At the time, it seemed the only thing I could do. I don't even know the details of how he handled it, but I do know he somehow bravely rid me of a most unwelcome suitor. Forbush really terrified me. I will be forever grateful to Robbie."

"And why did you not come to me?" Travis asked quietly.

Claire was mindful of Elizabeth's words. She hung her head, and finally decided to tell at the truth, or at least part of it.

"I think because I wanted him to be the one to solve the problem. I've grown fond of him."

She felt a little guilt that she was not telling the complete truth. But surely saving her brother's pride was more important. She felt some embarrassment divulging her feelings for Robbie, before he had shown any special regard for her. Still, she would rather sacrifice her own pride than insult Travis.

Travis had not expected her answer. It was something he couldn't quarrel with, even though he had an uneasy suspicion there was more to the story. Still, he knew his sister would never expose her feelings in such a manner unless they were genuine, and that this confession cost her a great deal. It cast a far different light on the matter. It also made sense of the interview Carstairs had asked him for the day before.

"Do you know he is soon leaving London? He informed me yesterday that his mother's health is improved, and he is leaving soon for Stramshire."

Again Claire's chin went up, and her eyes clouded.

"He has not told me. I wish he had."

"My dear girl," said Travis, "he told me in the context of informing me he hoped to be a formal suitor for your hand as soon as you've finished your season. He doesn't want to deprive you of all of the balls and routs, and especially of your coming-out party. I must confess I was surprised, and didn't take him too seriously. I was wrong, was I not? His feelings are very much to his credit, you know."

Claire's lovely face was aglow. Looking at her, her brother thought that he didn't have the whole story, but it might be wise to drop the matter. He had not previously considered Robbie as a suitor. His prospects were not what he envisioned for Claire. He was personable and honorable, and his lineage was impeccable, but it would be a long time before he advanced in the church hierarchy. That could be far in the future.

With an inward sigh, he stretched out his hands and Claire ran to him. He enfolded her in his arms and kissed the top of her head.

"Do not put yourself in the mopes, little one. All will come about."

Claire let herself be held for a long moment, clinging to the brother she adored. Then she kissed his cheek and quietly left. Both knew their exchange had been significant, and each wanted time to reflect. Travis looked after her, his face thoughtful. His little sister had ideas of her own, and her own brand of courage. He could not but applaud, even as he worried. She'd definitely have a say in her own future, as he would in no way force her.

He saw no reason to tell her that he and Robbie had also had a long discussion about Squire Bellamy, and that Robbie was going to be another guardian force for Kimberly and Elizabeth.

The next morning found Robbie paying a call on Elizabeth and Claire to announce his departure and make his goodbyes. Claire was glad Travis had given her warning, and sat demurely without betraying her feelings.

She sat so quietly that Robbie began to feel a little desperate, as he explained why he had to leave.

"For my mother is better, and I feel strongly I must return to my parish. My curate is a very good man, but he's not as eager as I for some of my programs, and I worry that some of the progress I made might be lost."

Claire looked up at that. "What kind of programs are you instigating, Mr. Carstairs?"

"I thought you had agreed to use my given name, Lady Claire. I would so like you to."

He smiled at her so winningly that she gave him such an encouraging smile he drew a deep breath.

"As to my programs, I am trying to set up a school for the younger boys and girls, and it's not going too well. The parents want the boys to work in the fields, but will consider some schooling, while they don't think girls need any educations at all. I have a few beginners, but I'm afraid my curate has let the classes slip."

"How I wish I could help," Claire said.

"How I wish you could," said Robbie. His voice was soft and tender, and seeing them both look at each other with undisguised admiration, Elizabeth begged to be excused to go find her embroidery material.

Neither Robbie nor Claire saw her go. Robbie moved to Claire, and taking both her hands in his, kissed first the back and then the palms. He felt the *frisson* of delight that ran through Claire, as he softly said, "I would not rob you of a moment of your come-out season. But if at the end of it, you are not committed to anyone, I'll reappear and hope you will regard my suit favorably. I ask for no promises, however. I have given my word to your brother, and to myself, that I will not rush you in any way."

Claire looked up into his dear face. It would be unfair to Travis to commit herself so early, but she had no intention of changing her mind. Still, she couldn't send him away without hope. She left her hands in his, and faced him with honesty and courage.

"I do not feel a season is as important to me as to some young ladies. I'll give you this promise. I will not make a commitment of any kind until I see you again."

Robbie beamed as he drew her hands close against his chest. "My sweet girl, that is more than I dared hope for."

Claire held tight to the hands that were holding hers.

"You don't think I'm too forward, do you?"

"My dear," Robbie said simply, "You are enchanting."

He gave her a brief and not altogether brotherly hug, kissed her hair, and said his goodbyes quickly. He did not trust himself to stay without pressing her for a firm promise, but that wouldn't do honor to himself or Travis.

Elizabeth finally returned, she found Claire smiling, but with eyes that were suspiciously bright.

"He is so very good," Claire said simply.

"You both are," said Elizabeth.

It seemed to be a day for hugging. Elizabeth fervently hoped these two dear people would be able to work their way through the obstacles they would surely be facing. While London society might regard a marriage between them as a *misalliance,* Elizabeth thought they couldn't be more perfectly suited.

Chapter Twenty-Two

ELIZABETH WAS NOT AS sanguine for her own chances of happiness as she was for Claire's. She no longer had any feeling of rapport and communication with Travis. Somehow, he'd distanced himself. It was a distance both physical and intellectual, and she dreadfully missed the easy camaraderie they had shared. He wouldn't even play chess with her, most politely regretting he was too busy.

She decided to try and understand him, and so started rising earlier than usual, hoping to catch him alone in the breakfast room. For several mornings she had been unsuccessful, and then one morning, when she entered the breakfast room she found him there. He greeted her pleasantly, but in short order picked up his paper and walked out, leaving most of his food on his plate.

She spent time thinking up conversational topics that had once interested them both. He was always courteous, almost excessively so, she could not crack the shell he'd erected around himself. His manners were impeccable, but he bore little resemblance to the man she'd laughed with and teased, and who'd enjoyed hearing her viewpoints on a variety of subjects. She couldn't understand why he'd changed to this degree. And she regretted it deeply.

David continued to be a frequent caller, and while she liked him very much indeed, he aroused not a scintilla of the feeling Travis roused with just a smiling glance. She gave David no overt encouragement, and he was clever enough to often include Claire in his invitations.

One afternoon, David had just finished handing Claire into the carriage, and held out his hand to Elizabeth. They saw Travis coming down the steps, using his cane and heading toward Regent Street. His head was down and he didn't seem to notice them. David looked at him with a puzzled frown, and then shrugged and started to hand Elizabeth up.

Before they could get in the carriage, they both paused as they saw Travis stop to speak to a small girl selling oranges. She was ragged and barefoot, and Travis had his hand in his pocket even while he talked to her.

"How like him," Elizabeth murmured. "He'll probably empty his purse for the child. But she's only a baby, David."

"Like many a street child. She's probably got someone pushing her onto the streets for his own benefit."

Even as they watched, a burly man, even filthier than the child, appeared in the background, watching eagerly as Travis handed his entire purse to the child, murmuring something to her. The child looked up with adoration, clutching the purse in both hands and evidently uttering her thanks.

Travis turned and limped away. The brute in the background, perhaps thinking it was safe to do whatever he wanted since Travis was crippled, moved in and grabbed at the purse. The child screamed in protest, clutching the money. As David and Elizabeth watched, the bully slapped her so hard she fell to the ground.

David rushed to pick her up, Elizabeth screamed, and Travis turned to limp back as fast as he could. Even as Elizabeth watched, Travis flung his cane aside to attack the brute, who drew his knife and slashed out viciously. Travis tried to twist away, and the wicked knife missed his chest but slashed him from hip to knee, and he plunged to the ground.

The little girl seemed rooted to the spot in terror.

Elizabeth rushed to Travis and knelt beside him, thankful the brute had run from the scene.

"My love," she said, "You are so very brave, and I only hope you've escaped serious harm."

"The child?" he murmured.

"Is well and unhurt. We'll take her home with us."

Travis gave her a very sweet smile, and then slowly closed his eyes and lost consciousness. Startled, her eyes swept his body. For the first time she noticed that his previously injured leg was split open from knee to hip in a wickedly deep cut. Blood was pumping from the wound at an alarming rate.

She sprang to her feet in terror, looking for someone to help her hold the wound closed, and found David beside her. He was panting from exertion, and she could only suppose he'd been chasing the brute. He must have caught him, as his knuckles were bruised and bleeding and he'd been smiling when he first appeared.

"Elizabeth, my dear, calm yourself. We will send for a surgeon immediately. Will you and Claire get a room ready on the first floor? Also send Phillips to me. We will need strips of cloth so we can staunch the bleeding. Then we will carry Travis gently into the house."

Elizabeth turned and ran up the stone steps, leaving Claire to follow hurriedly. Jamieson had the door open before she reached it, and told her he'd already sent a maid for cloths. Elizabeth thought of when his maddened horse had brought Travis low, and how he had suffered for so many days before he recovered. Surely this was much worse! How could he endure another setback?

Seizing a handful of cloths she hurried to David, who was trying to hold the terrible wound closed with his hands. Tearing off strips, she handed them to him and he bound one after another tightly around the upper thigh. By this time David also was splattered with blood. He dried his hands as best he could with a scrap of cloth. He motioned to Phillips to take Travis' head while he took the feet.

"At least this way we can keep the upper part of his body unstained," David said grimly. "I pray his mother is not at home."

The two men straightened, jarring Travis as little as possible, and began a slow journey up the steps and into the house. Jamieson had prepared a bed on a sofa in the parlor, and they carried him there. Fortunately the doctor arrived almost immediately, and did a quick examination of his head and upper body. He then looked at the leg, but did not touch it.

"He is not injured except for this gash, as far as I can see, but it must be closed immediately. Will one of you help me get some laudanum down him?"

Travis opened his eyes and murmured weakly, but clearly, "No laudanum."

Lady Rivington and Claire were now standing in the doorway, frozen in terror.

"All of you ladies must leave," said the doctor. "I need no distractions from vaporish females."

As the doctor again bent over Travis, Phillips stayed, and David went to the ladies, whispering reassurances, and guiding them from the room.

The doctor turned to Elizabeth. "You too, madam," he said firmly.

Elizabeth lifted her chin and glared at him. "I will not leave unless you carry me out, and then I would return. I advise you to help your patient. I will not yield on this."

The doctor glanced at Phillips, who gave a slight shrug. The doctor glowered at her and then turned to his patient.

"If you faint on me, madam, I will not even pick you up. At least try to stay out of the way."

He was soon very grateful she had stayed, for she moved to Travis' side, and taking her hand in his, spoke softly, but with determination.

"I am not leaving, my lord, until the stitching of your leg is completed to my satisfaction. But if you do not have a care for yourself, will you take pity on me? It will be so much easier for me if you take just a little of the laudanum and I don't have to watch the worst of your suffering. And perhaps some brandy, as well?"

Travis made the barest attempt at a smile.

"Is there any way I can persuade you to leave?"

"None," she said sweetly.

"You are most ungenerous, Elizabeth. You know I would not make it worse for you." He smiled faintly and turned to the doctor. "Do as the wily lady says, doctor," he whispered. "Bring on the hateful stuff."

He swallowed the dose and then lay back, white and still. Elizabeth did not know if he had fainted again, or if the laudanum could possibly work that quickly. She moved to the bedside, determined to keep her eye on every move the doctor made.

She was pleasantly surprised that she didn't have to insist that the doctor thoroughly wash his hands. She did also, and asked Phillips to do the same. The laudanum was beginning to take effect, but knew the wound had to be cleansed, and that this lethargy would not completely obliterate Travis' agony. Nevertheless, she was glad the doctor was conscientious in the cleansing, finishing by pouring brandy over the wound, not once, but twice.

Elizabeth held Travis' hand tightly, and he returned the grip tenfold. He did not make a sound, but the strength of his hold showed his pain. The bones in Elizabeth's hand were crushed and throbbing, but she didn't attempt to wiggle free. The doctor pulled out his stitching materials, and then stopped, peering into the gaping wound. He grabbed his forceps and reached in, extracting some tiny pieces of metal. He then motioned Phillips to stand by to hold Travis down, and picked up his needle again.

Travis did not need to be held down. Although he whitened to an alarming degree, he did not move, nor did he make a sound. His grip on Elizabeth's hand became even more painful, but she didn't falter. It seemed to all of them a nightmarish time before the doctor finished.

"There," he said, straightening up. He wiped his hands, and then held out a dish with the three small pieces of metal, one slightly bigger than the others.

"Please give these to his lordship when he recovers. These little bits of Frenchie's handiwork must have been causing him agony. He might want to save them for his grandchildren."

The painful wound closed, Travis let the laudanum take over, and lapsed into a deep sleep. Elizabeth and Phillips stared at each other. The mental chips were doubtless from the bullet the army doctors had not been able to completely remove. Elizabeth's face suddenly blazed with hope.

The surgeon finished wrapping the leg and gave a sigh of satisfaction.

"That's a fine job of stitching, if I do say so." Wiping his brow, he looked at the white faces of Phillips and Elizabeth. "Come, come, that was not easy, but you were both splendid, and you, madam, were magnificent. The Earl should rest for a while, but when he awakens, he must be kept quiet until the leg has a chance to heal. I suggest you set up a watch you can depend upon, so that someone's always with him. He must not be allowed to thrash around. If no infection sets in, he will soon be on the road to recovery. Call me immediately, however, if his temperature rises. Do anything you have to do to keep him quiet. He seems to favor the young lady's company. I suggest she get some rest now so she can be on hand when he awakens."

He bade a courteous goodnight to them all, including David who had rejoined the party during the stitching. It was a subdued David, and not only because he truly hated seeing Travis suffer. The accident had clarified his thinking in a not too surprising way.

Elizabeth's reaction had clearly shown her love for Travis. He now realized he had little chance with her. Whether she knew the depth of her feelings, and whether Travis would ever declare himself, he did not know. They were both his dear friends, and he would stand by them while they faced a most uncertain future. His own plans no longer mattered.

Chapter Twenty-Three

THE FOLLOWING MORNING found Travis still somewhat under the effects of the laudanum, but beginning to stir restlessly. Elizabeth fashioned a tent of two pillows, one on each side of his injured leg, so that the bedding was not rubbing against the fearsome wound. David had stayed with him through the night, stretched out in a large armchair.

David was sent to bed, and the ladies decided to take turns, with his mother and Claire taking the first shift. Elizabeth had slept an anxious few hours, and forced herself to eat some breakfast. She longed to be with Travis every moment, but knew she mustn't infringe on his family's rights.

She'd almost finished eating when the maid rushed in, saying Claire had sent for her. She tossed down her napkin and dashed to the sickroom.

Claire met her at the doorway, her eyes and voice frantic.

"He does not hear me, Elizabeth! He keeps trying to sit up, and I know he should not. Maybe your voice will calm him."

Elizabeth drew a chair close to the bed, taking his hand in one of hers, and soothing his forehead with the other.

"Dear Travis," she said, "pray don't distress yourself so. Your leg has suffered a temporary setback, but I truly believe it will soon be better than ever."

He showed no signs of understanding her, but her voice seemed to have a soothing effect. He settled back. But as soon as she stopped speaking, he began to toss. So she continued talking of anything and everything that came into her mind. The minute she was quiet he began thrashing.

On the pretext of feeling his forehead she smoothed back his disheveled hair, something she had long wanted to do. His forehead was warm, but not distressingly so. She kept talking to him soothingly for several hours, drawing on stories of her own childhood, telling him of Richard's, saying anything she could think of to keep him still. She doubted that she even made sense.

Her voice was hoarse, but she was happier than she had been in some time. The fact he needed her, and that even though only partially conscious, wanted her with him, was a delight after his recent coldness. If his leg indeed improved, perhaps his worries would ease and they could be back on their old easy footing. She'd missed his teasing stimulation so very much.

The surgeon came every day to check Lord Cade's leg.

"Well, my lord, I am very pleased you're not running a fever."

This was on the third day after the accident. "Now let me take a look at my beautiful embroidery." With a chuckle he bared the leg. "Capital, capital, sir. There is not a mark of undue infection. While this will take some time to heal, you will soon be up and about. Let me not hear of you leaving this bed for a fortnight. This is a very large wound, and will need that much time at the least. You can be very thankful I'm not of the school that bleeds my patients, as you'd already lost a deal of blood. In fact, I think I will add red wine to your diet. Much better than leeches, in my opinion."

Turning to Elizabeth, he added, "Give him what he wants in the way of food and drink, but do not let him get agitated in any manner. We are off to a good start. Let's keep it that way."

As the doctor left, Elizabeth turned to find Travis looking at her gravely.

"I think you have been with me most of the time. Is that not so?"

Elizabeth flushed, partly from embarrassment, and partly from pleasure that he sounded perfectly lucid, and in this world again.

"We have all taken turns, my lord. Let me call your mother. She has been excessively worried."

"I would have your hand, Elizabeth," he said softly, holding out his own. She came to the bed quickly, and was almost overcome when he took her hand and carried it to his lips, lingering over the caress. It was only his way of saying thanks, she told herself; still, it felt so good to have him touch her. Her heart pounded in her ears as his eyes blazed up at her. There was palpable tension in the air, and she knew by the way he dropped his eyelids to cover the intensity of his gaze that he was well aware of it. She forced herself to take a deep breath.

"Now you may call my mother. I wanted to thank you first. I think your presence has been most necessary to me."

"You quite put me out of countenance. I did nothing we didn't all do. But I'll not argue today. The doctor himself said we must not gainsay you. You'll get excessively spoiled."

She dimpled at him and went to summon his mother, leaving Travis looking thoughtfully after her.

His leg, though it hurt abominably, was not the same excruciating pain that he'd known for so long. It was rather an all-over ache. One that could be expected from having a large wound cleansed and stitched. He remembered through haze of the agonizing stitching, that the doctor had said something about removing some bullet fragments. Looking at the bedside table, he did indeed see some small pieces of metal in a dish. Could it be that his long and agonizing disability might be attributed to those tiny scraps? He was afraid to hope, and closing his eyes, drifted off into an uneasy slumber. Yet his thoughts, plus Elizabeth's charming confusion when he'd lingered over the kiss to her palm, sent him to sleep with a smile on his lips.

THE ATMOSPHERE OF CADE House somehow became charged with optimism. His family did not speak of their hope, beyond a few circumspect words. Yet all of them were praying that as Travis recovered, his debilitating war injury would be healed along with the new one. The servants, even though they didn't know the details, knew that something was buoying the spirits of the ladies of the house. Phillips could have told them the whole story, but would never betray the confidence of his master. Besides, he was superstitious about jinxing what might be a providential stroke of luck.

Yet there were extra smiles from everyone as Travis gradually regained his strength.

There was certainly no shortage of people to do the Earl's bidding. His servants knew him not only as a war hero but also as a fair and just master. His mother and sister would have devoted every minute to him, if he would have permitted it. However, without it being expressly stated, it became accepted that the Earl was happiest when Miss Elizabeth tended him.

Everyone helped her have extra time. When needed, Lady Rivington and Aunt Lavinia chaperoned Claire. Often David stood in as escort, so that

Elizabeth was free to be with Travis or to pursue interests that refreshed her. Travis insisted that she have an hour or so each day for herself.

Elizabeth relished her privileged position. She read to Travis, and when he could be propped up against his pillows, they played chess. Sometimes he dozed with half-closed eyes. At these times, if she made a restless movement, his eyelids flew open. She learned to sit quietly. As he grew stronger she began reading aloud from the daily newspapers. The war news was somewhat better, with Napoleon in difficulty in his retreat from Russia, and Wellington entering France after regrouping his forces following the battle of Vittoria.

Elizabeth felt a new buoyancy, and when she was not with Travis, found delight in the unusual joy of time alone. She'd been told emphatically she was to do nothing but amuse herself when not with Travis. Since she had long wanted to explore the city, she took her maid and went on short explorations. London was so interesting that she wondered how much of her enthusiasm was due to the city and how much to her hopes for Travis. She stored up topics of conversation. Gas lit lamps had begun to replace the old oil lamps on London's street. J.M.W. Turner exhibited his wondrous canvas of Hannibal Crossing the Alps, and Elizabeth was moved to tears when she first saw his original and colorful style. Everything was intensely exciting to her, and she longed for the day when she could share such expeditions with Travis, not just tell him about them.

In the meantime, their conversations ranged ever wider and more satisfying.

One day, she sat watching him lay an elaborate trap for her king.

"My lord Earl, you are most unfair. You are supposed to be in ill health and therefore to be easy pickings."

Travis merely smiled at her. He had just blocked her from passing one of her pawns for a queen, and was waiting to see what enchantingly intelligent move she would make next.

They had finished discussing Lord Byron's *Childe Harold's Pilgrimage*, which each felt was too flowery for his tastes. Elizabeth held out strongly for his originality.

"I am surprised, Elizabeth," Travis said. "A proper young lady shouldn't be so fascinated by a poet of Lord Byron's reputation."

"Nonsense," said Elizabeth. "You don't even mean that. There is nothing prim about you, so don't try to bait me. Byron has the chance of turning into a first class poet, if he resists society's temptations."

He watched as she pondered her next move. The sun through the window shone on her gleaming head, and bathed her face with light when she raised it to glance at him. He thought he had never seen such a captivating sight. It was one of the times when he could gaze at her safely, without revealing his love. She was looking to find a way to move her queen out of danger, and so missed his intense gaze.

He turned to a subject that had long been on his mind. "Elizabeth, have you ever thought you might want a season of your own? I'd be more than pleased if you would let me present you and Claire at the same time. Your birth entitles you, and I would love to do so. I know you've never wanted to ask your grandfather to stand sponsor, but would you let me?"

Elizabeth turned a deep shade of rose and positively glared.

"I would never countenance such a thing, as you must know. I'm surprised you even suggest it."

There was no doubt she was offended, and Travis cursed his lack of adroitness.

"As to our grandfather, he has never acknowledged Richard or me. We did not exist, once he had disowned his son for marrying out of the *ton*. I would not go to him for aid at my father's death, and I will not now."

"And Richard?" Travis asked. "Might he not one day want to know his grandfather?"

"I've thought of that many times," she said. "And have you thought that perhaps he wouldn't be the charming boy he is if he'd had the material advantages our grandfather withheld? When he gets older, he can make up his own mind. But only when he is strong enough to stand up to a man who must be the antithesis of everything he and I treasure."

"Besides," she continued, "I have never wanted to be in society. The preoccupation with clothes, the lack of purpose, the constant gossip; I do not want that as a way of my life. Most of my enjoyment here in London has come because I feel I've found true friends. Your mother, Claire, and even David seem to me to be real people. The others are merely figures on a brightly lit, but artificial stage."

Travis again found himself looking at the top of her gleaming head.

"Elizabeth," he said. "Surely you know that above all else I want the best for you."

She kept her head bowed. Her thoughts seemed so loud that she wondered if he could hear them. Did not he know that he alone was the best for her? That nothing and no one would ever surpass him?

"Tell me what you have heard from Richard," he asked, as she remained silent. He hated it when she would not look at him.

She could not help grinning a little as she usually did when discussing Richard.

"His latest letter tells me about one of his classmates he is not fond of. Other than this one bully, Richard seems popular, and he certainly loves the school. I know you have kept up with his educational progress and are satisfied. I'm not worried about his eventually handling the bully, but it'll be interesting to see how he goes about it."

"You are wise to trust Richard," said Travis with a grin of his own.

The doctor came daily, and seemed very pleased with his patient's progress. After one week Travis insisted on getting out of bed, if only to walk to the nearest chair. When the time came to remove the stitches, Travis requested politely that everyone, even Phillips, leave the room.

"And what is on your mind, my lord?" asked Dr. Brainard as he adeptly worked at his task.

Travis gave a short laugh. "You are most perceptive. First, I'd like your opinion of the pieces of shot you took from my leg. The former pain I knew so well has disappeared. Can I count on it being truly gone?"

"I rather expected that question, which I'll answer as best I can. The pieces of shot must have caused you agonizing pain if they came in contact with certain nerves. To be sure their removal is most positive. I cannot, however, promise that I got them all, I did not see any more, and your wound was wide and gaping. I think you are probably cured, but only time will give you a true answer."

Travis looked at him thoughtfully. An honest man, the doctor. There had, indeed, been no more of the pain he'd come to take for granted, but he was afraid to hope too much until he was on his feet and active.

"And the second reason you wanted to see me alone?" Dr. Brainard smiled gently, smoothing the bedcovers back over his noble patient's leg.

Travis looked at him directly.

"I have a most particular question to ask you about another matter. I see no way to lead up to it gently. As a medical man, can you tell me if it is possible for a lady to lose her maidenhead without any sign of bleeding?"

"Ah. That is indeed a very particular question." The doctor started packing up his medical bag.

"I have no difficulty in answering it, however. First, it's not at all general, but a few young women seem to have never had a maidenhead. Second, if a lady has led an active life she can have breeched her maidenhead inadvertently. I recall one case where a husband came to me, about to set his wife aside thinking she had betrayed him before their marriage. She was a horsewoman who was given to riding astride, and I persuaded him he had no true cause to suspect her of infidelity. Does this answer your question?"

Travis looked even more thoughtful. "Yes, it does. I thank you for your honesty, as well as your conscientious care of me. Did the marriage you speak of work its way out of such suspicions?"

Dr. Brainard snapped his case shut. "They are still together, and I hope he trusts her. She is a sweet and virtuous lady. Good-bye, my lord. I will call again in a few days to check that your wound is not pulling apart, but it should not. However, exercise caution for a few more days."

Travis sat very still. He had the answer he'd both anticipated and dreaded. It was probable his vivid dream of Elizabeth in his arms had been real. He remembered how they'd ridden together over the fields of Kimberly. She'd habitually ridden astride, garbed in cut-down breeches of her father's. She had looked charming, and very sensibly unconventional. The breeches enhanced her figure to a remarkable degree.

He feared he'd acted shamefully. He must be more than ever careful he did nothing further to compromise her. In addition, he'd alerted his whole family to his deep feelings for her, with his constant demands for her presence. He closed his eyes with regret. It was time to end their treasured intimacy. He'd been weak to allow it to continue this long. He hoped she had no idea how she set his pulse racing whenever she entered the room. His loins tightened every time he let himself look at her. The need to bury his hands in her hair and drag her face to his and let loose all the raging passion he'd felt for so long was always present.

So far he thought he'd covered up fairly well. Still, he was not being fair to her. He couldn't yet know what his future would be.

He must double his efforts to remain aloof until he knew.

Chapter Twenty-Four

AS TRAVIS REGAINED strength, he made it plain to one and all that he wanted time alone. True, he'd let the estate affairs slide, and needed badly to have his man of business bring him up to date. That, of course, was not the real reason, and from the hurt look on Elizabeth's face, she suspected his withdrawal was deliberate.

He put Elizabeth from his mind as much as possible, sternly jerking his thoughts to other topics if they started to stray back to her. Still, she'd woven herself so firmly into the fabric of his life that almost everything he did reminded him of her. He sat in his study one morning, going over his mail, and discarding all the invitations and solicitations to be dealt with later. At an envelope with unfamiliar writing, but with the return address of Stramshire, he came to attention. He opened and glanced quickly at the signature of Robert Carstairs.

Dear Lord Cade;

I am writing on the matter you asked me to monitor. I think our friend Squire Bellamy is planning more mischief. Crawley and I have agreed I would be the one to keep you informed, as writing is difficult for him.

Two strangers have appeared in town, once again asking questions about Kimberly. If you wish to send a Runner down again, it might be wise, but I think we have the matter in hand. Crawley, (an excellent man, by the way) and his two main helpers, Bright and Hawkins, are very much on the alert. They've taken to wandering down to the pub nightly and are slowly getting to be drinking companions of the strangers. It seems the strangers are also courting their acquaintance, as they've confided they hope to be hired as stable hands at Kimberly.

Bright and Hawkins are pretending to be friendly, so we have an entry into the enemy camp, so to speak.

I will keep you advised.

As ever, your sincere servant,
Robert Carstairs.

Travis sat a long time over the letter, holding it lightly in his hand, and perusing it more than once. He had no doubt that Kimberly was in danger, and in a way that could devastate Elizabeth. While he had arranged with his man of business that she and Richard would always have a more than adequate income, he knew that money would never compensate for devastation at Kimberly.

He longed to go down himself, but knew he could not. Not only was his strength not yet up to par, but the sight of him would make Squire Bellamy instantly aware that his plans were in danger. What he needed was to discover Bellamy's plot and frustrate it in a manner that would totally implicate the blasted Squire.

Things could not be in better hands than Carstairs and Crawley. He would have to rely on them. He penned a short note of thanks to Carstairs, and requested frequent communication.

Two days later another letter arrived.

My lord Travis;

I am certain you wish me to keep you almost daily advised. We have made some progress in that the pub keeper suddenly decided why he thought one of the strangers seemed familiar. He states that without the dark dye on his hair, and newly grown moustache, he would be a ringer for the previous stranger suspected of being the arsonist. It seems Squire Bellamy has not given up.

The strangers have asked if Bright and Hawkins can help them obtain work at Kimberly, stating that they have heard how fair the steward is, and that there's plenty of work that needs to be done, and at good wages. Our men have stalled so far, but we are all beginning to think we will not get to the bottom of this unless we take a chance and hire them. Needless to say they would be watched, nay, more than watched, scrutinized, at all times.

If you have an objection to this plan please send word immediately. Otherwise I think it is the direction we will take. They must certainly not be allowed near the stables.

Your servant, sir,
Carstairs.

Again Travis sat reading and re-reading the letter. How he longed to jump on Palisades and ride hell for leather till he reached Kimberly. As it was, he could do little but agree that the chance must be taken of letting the villains openly on the property. It would be much better to know where they were at all times. Still, he could not like it.

Not at all!

He tried to put himself in Bellamy's shoes. The man nursed a malignant hatred of both Elizabeth and Travis, and would try to hurt them in the most shocking way he could imagine. He must try to think the way a vindictive madman would think, if he wished to forestall him. Travis feared very much for the horses. The Runner he had dispatched should be at Kimberly by now, and with all of them alert, surely tragedy could be averted. Once again he cursed the fact that he was not the man he had once been, although he cherished the hope he could regain his former strength and power.

Travis sat down immediately and dashed off a short note to Robbie.

Carstairs,

I agree with all you are doing. I know I need not urge you to always have a man with each of this pair, and to keep them separated. On no account must they be allowed near the stables.

With thanks and deep obligation,

Travis.

He sighed, and steepling his hands, sat for a long time trying to think of anything he might have missed. Thank God Elizabeth knew nothing of this.

Over a week passed before the next communication.

"My lord Travis," began Robbie, "*the crisis is over, but it was a very near thing. As we all agreed, someone was always with the two new hired hands, and they were not allowed near the stables. We were most particular that they were never working together in any situation. Since we now know their real names, I will call them Sims, who is the known arsonist, and Weldon, who was his accomplice.*

This morning, Bright was watching Weldon's work group, which was several fields away from Hawkins and Sims and their group. Suddenly Weldon swung his hoe at Bright's knees, and took off running across the fields. Hawkins, seeing that Bright could not pursue, struggled to his feet and began to chase the runaway. This was of course the reaction Sims wanted, and he headed for the stables at a dead run. The other workers, knowing nothing of our suspicions and under no instructions, watched in amazement.

Crawley and your Runner, Evans, had previously agreed that in any emergency Crawley would immediately go to guard the stables and Evans the house. We were all still worried about fire. But this time the plot was even more nefarious. Crawley let Sims enter the stables, hoping to catch him in the act of arson, and quickly followed. Instead, he found Sims with Blue Fire's left rear leg in one hand, and a wicked knife in the other. Sims freely admits he intended to hamstring the horse. Crawley was quick enough to put a gun to his head, and told him he was a dead man unless he dropped the knife. He did so with a sneer, and no sign of regret. Evans, who is a genius at questioning, soon got him to admit that Bellamy was behind it all, and had promised Sims not only a large sum of money, but immunity from prosecution.

I was able to convince him that my father would have another magistrate in place immediately, and that he'd made a grave error in offending both the Earl of Darby and the Earl of Cade. He had not known of the involvement of such high personages. The end result is that we struck a bargain with him. In exchange for a charge of crime that will bring him deportation against one asking for the gallows, he has signed a written statement that completely ruins Bellamy. I trust this meets with your approval.

Bellamy has not been in these parts for several days. Doubtless he planned to be far way from the horrible mutilation of two beautiful animals. Oh yes, Sims had instruction to also hamstring Firebird. The Runners are looking for Bellamy, but I doubt if they find him, as he certainly won't return.

Sims is under lock and key. I have mixed feelings about Weldon. I believe him when he says he thought he was helping only in a theft. He was aghast, and I think sincerely, to hear the true plan. He is an ex-soldier who has found no work for the six months since his return from the war, and has a hungry wife and small child living under the hedgerows.

If you consent, I will send him to one of my father's more remote holdings to work. I see no gain in having him languish in prison while his family starves. I think him essentially a good man who was driven to desperation.

Please give me your thoughts on this.

I believe the danger to Kimberly to be finally over.

I am ever your servant, my dear sir.

Carstairs.

Travis sat long over this communication, reading and re-reading it until he almost had it memorized. He would have to give an expurgated version to Elizabeth, emphasizing only that all was well and that Robbie had been of inestimable help. He thanked God for both Robbie and Crawley. He thought wryly that if Robbie appeared at that moment demanding his sister's hand, his proposal would be accepted instantly. Indeed, Robbie was an exemplary man, generous in his praise of others, conspicuously brave, and scrupulous in his honesty. Any woman would be lucky to have him.

After carefully pondering how to render his account of the recent events, he went to find Elizabeth. He resolved to calm any doubts she might have, but to do so in a detached manner. He must cushion her from the future shock of his leaving. It was desperately hard to treat her with indifference. And there was still Claire's ball to get through.

Chapter Twenty-Five

PLANS FOR THE BALL absorbed every member of the household except Travis. Claire was to be formally presented to society, and it seemed all of society had accepted the invitations to attend. The amount of work needed to bring about one young lady's presentation astonished Elizabeth. Most of the addressing of envelopes for the ball had been done during Travis' last illness. Now there was the decision of the select fifty that would be invited to dinner before the ball, and those more intimate invitations to be issued. Plus there were catering arrangements for both the dinner and the late supper at the ball, menus to be chosen, and a truly staggering amount of consultation over the wines. Travis relented and gave his advice on this important selection.

Decisions must be made as to rooms for cards, retiring rooms, and cloakrooms. Extra servants must be borrowed or hired. The task of decorating the ballroom, not used for many years, was formidable. Hundreds of wax candles were inserted into the newly scrubbed and glistening chandeliers. Elizabeth had suggested that the flowers be confined to white roses, to compliment Claire's blonde loveliness, and the day of the ball, armloads of roses arrived not only from the Rivington forcing houses, but from the town florists. White and silver flocked sarcenet draped the tall windows.

For her ball, Claire was dressed in white with a pink underskirt. Her hair cascaded in curls over one shoulder, with the rest drawn up and secured with a pearl tiara. She wore the Rivington pearls around her neck, which Travis had given her the morning of the ball. Elizabeth had artfully applied a slight amount of burnt cork to Claire's eyebrows and lashes, so that her beautiful eyes looked even larger. Lady Rivington wasn't aware of the light makeup, but she agreed with everyone that Claire was in the best of looks.

The dinner party preceding the ball was impressive from its beginning, with the three chandeliers in the formal dining room reflecting light from the sparkling jewels worn by the ladies, and the gleaming array of silver on the table. A footman stood behind each chair. Lady Rivington's old friends were there, as well as the Branleigh twins and their parents, Viscount and Viscountess Litchfield. Of course Kingsley, Stokely, and Stanton were also in attendance. Elizabeth was delighted to see several members of the government present, and she noticed the foreign secretary, Lord Castlereagh, in conversation with Travis, was listening intently.

At the last minute Viscount and Viscountess Carstairs, and their son Robert, were admitted. Claire's surprised glow lit the room. Elizabeth flashed an inquiring look at Travis, who gave her a slow smile. Evidently Robbie was there by design, and with Travis' approval.

Travis' smile had been more intimate than his usual stoic countenance. Elizabeth felt her very insides melt, as they always did when he showed any sign of the closeness that she cherished. She entered the dining room on Kingsley's arm, already aglow, and determined to have a wonderful evening.

She couldn't begin to eat all the many removes the dinner offered. Venison, tongue, ham, and quail were presented, beside salmon and turbot. The ten courses were each accompanied by a different wine, and she marveled at the way most of the gentlemen not only ate much of the food, but drank a great deal of the wine. She very soon gave up even trying, and confined herself to conversation, merely sipping at her wine, and waving the footman away when he tried to refill her glass.

At the end of the meal Travis rose to salute his sister with champagne.

"Most of you already know my beautiful sister, Claire, and agree with me that society is blessed to welcome her to its ranks. I would not change her in any particular. Lords and ladies, let us drink to Claire."

It was a decidedly merry party that showed its pleasure at the toast. Elizabeth noted that Robbie raised his glass in salute, touching it to his lips, with his eyes fastened on Claire's. Of course she was blushing from the attention, but she returned Robbie's glance as steadily as he offered it.

The huge ballroom on the second floor was starting to fill with people, and Lady Rivington, Claire, and Lord Cade took up their positions on the staircase to welcome the guests. As the first strains of music appeared, Travis led his sister onto the dance floor. Elizabeth held her breath, not knowing if his leg had healed enough for him to dance. He was still limping slightly, but his walk was much steadier.

He must have had the same doubts, as David appeared and claimed Claire for the first set. David, with his shock of prematurely gray hair, strong and elegant in a navy blue velvet evening ensemble, and Claire, alight with excitement, blond and truly beautiful on this her night, made a striking couple. Murmurs could be heard commenting on how handsome and well-suited they were. But when Robbie claimed Claire for the second dance, her face lit with joy. It was apparent to everyone she was giving him her heart along with her hand. Elizabeth looked at them with pleasure, and turned quickly to see Travis looking not at all disconcerted. Lady Rivington and Lord and Lady Darby beamed at them, and Elizabeth doubted very much if Claire had more than one season. She hoped Lord Stokely would not be too disappointed.

She gave a small sigh and turned to find Travis beside her.

"You are truly beautiful tonight, Elizabeth," he stated quietly. His eyes were warm, and she thought he was looking at her as if she were a valuable painting. She did not want to be a painting on the wall. She wanted this man to hold her as a treasure, but in his strong arms. She was afraid if he caught even a glimmer of her feelings he'd turn and leave. He retreated so quickly from her approaches.

She spoke as lightly as she could. "I wondered when you led Claire out if you intended to try the dance. I would wager you could have done it. Your step is so much firmer. Is much of the pain gone?"

He smiled down at her.

"Other than the slight ache from my mostly healed wound, I have no pain. I would not, however, risk dancing for the first time in so many years in front of all of London."

"Perhaps you should have joined Claire and me in our lessons," she said teasingly. He continued to stare at her, an intensity in his eyes that puzzled her.

"Robbie and Claire are a handsome couple. Are you reconciled to a match between them, Travis?"

"Oh, I have long been reconciled, Elizabeth. More than that, I have come to think they are excellently suited. Claire would never be happy leading the vacuous life of a noblewoman dedicated to the empty pleasures of the *ton*. With Robbie she will feel useful, and I now know that's most necessary to her. I've recently learned, although Carstairs does not yet know it, that his father is obtaining the additional living of the adjoining parish for him. That will give them a large group of parishioners to help, and I imagine they will revel in it."

His tone was light, but she thought it got a little more earnest as he continued.

"And you, Elizabeth, are you reconciled?"

Elizabeth could not even imagine what he meant until she remembered she had once told him of Robbie's interest in her. She shook her head in disbelief.

"Travis, I am delighted for them. Who could not be? When I go home it will be wonderful to have them both nearby."

He looked at her sharply but did not say anything. Her heart sank, as he made no comment about her leaving. She forced herself to continue brightly.

"Did you know Robbie is trying to begin a small school that will teach not only the local boys, but some of the girls? Claire could truly be a help to him in that. I think they will have a fight on their hands. Most of the farmers see no reason their children should read and write. He's started with only a few boys, but they'll have a battle with the other parents."

"I don't doubt they'll win the battle," Travis said calmly. "They will make a dedicated and irresistible pair."

They stood quietly for a while, watching the dancing couples. He did not speak, and the silence was peaceful. For the first time in weeks, Elizabeth felt in harmony with him, a feeling of being so in one with his thoughts that no words were necessary. It was the most wonderful feeling in the world, she thought. She would be content to stand here forever, by his side, with an inner conviction that this was how it should be.

Travis turned, smiling, and held out his hands to her.

"Will you come with me for a short time? I would like you to go to the library with me."

She never hesitated, simply placing her hand lightly on his proffered arm. She would go anyplace he requested. He led her down the steps to the library, now deserted, but softly lit by candles and a cheerful fire. Even though it was almost summer, this room had not yet completely shed its winter's chill. Travis spent a good deal of time here, and had ordered a fire to be always laid. The fire cast a soft glow around the room that Elizabeth had always loved. It looked welcoming, and warm.

As he ushered her into the room, Travis spoke in a low tone she had never heard from him. Just his voice sent shivers up and down her body that made her look at him in astonishment.

"I will not take a chance of compromising you, Elizabeth, so we will leave the door well open. I do, however, dearly wish to waltz at least once with you."

He was looking at her with the look she'd longed for. A yearning look that made her feel beautiful, desirable, and cherished, all the things she wanted so badly to be for him. She slowly smiled as she realized they were directly under the ballroom, and the strains of a waltz were floating down.

"How wonderful," she breathed. "That you are well enough to waltz, and that you want to waltz with me."

Travis took her lightly in his arms, his right hand firmly at her waist. Elizabeth had never danced the waltz with any man but her dancing teacher, and this was different indeed. She suddenly understood why their elders considered it a dangerous dance. Travis held her tenderly, with an easy grace, but pulling her more and more closely to him. She could feel his body as they twirled and swayed, his hard firmness so different from her own softness, his scent a pleasing mixture of masculinity, cologne, and cleanliness that was his alone. His hand moved to the small of her back as he drew her yet closer, pressing her to him, and she easily followed his movements. She felt as if her very bones were melting in the surge of his heat. His hand at her waist seemed to be branding her. He was holding her so close she thought she might well go up in flames.

He was a superb dancer, in spite of his doubts. It was exhilarating to effortlessly follow his lead. They might have been dancing together for years, it seemed so easy to move with him. He drew her even nearer, bringing her hand to his chest in an intimate gesture that arched her body against his.

She dreamily swayed in his arms, and then, opening her eyes, found that the music had stopped. They stood for a moment in silence, and then he carefully withdrew his arm from her waist. She instinctively tried to draw close again, to keep and treasure the wonder she had been experiencing. He looked down at her, his eyes hooded, and then he took her face in both his hands, and lowered his lips to hers. The kiss was deep and sweet, and lasted until they both needed to breathe. Even then, he lifted his lips only to trail kisses across her face, and then came back to her eager mouth.

Her arms were around his neck, and she tried to tighten them even as she felt him once again pull away. He swung his body from hers, turning his back to her, and she saw that his shoulders were heaving. His voice was unsteady as he spoke.

"I should say I am sorry, but I am not. But I should not have touched you. It was not well done of me."

To her utter astonishment, he started to walk away. At the door he turned and looked at her with both regret and sorrow on his face.

"Forgive me if you can, Elizabeth. I shall not soon forgive myself."

A sense of profound desolation left her trembling as she stood alone. To leave her unescorted would be anathema to his impeccable courtesy. It was so unlike him that she had no idea how to interpret this last action. It certainly made no sense of the marvelous intimacy she thought they'd enjoyed.

The ball was but half over, and she must return to the ballroom. If both Travis and she disappeared for the rest of the evening, she knew well the gossip it would cause. She made her way back to the ballroom. Robbie, Claire and David were in a vivacious discussion, and she was grateful that they did not even pause in their conversation, but welcomed her into it. Only David gave her a searching look before lightly putting her hand on his arm and patting it. She felt in a haze, a nightmarish miasma that thickened as it became apparent Travis had disappeared from the ball. His mother and Claire looked around the crowded room from time to time, but no one mentioned his name. Elizabeth thought that good manners sometimes came in very handy.

Elizabeth danced with all her promised partners, laughing and teasing with them. She could not have told you a single name of those she had danced with, nor a word she'd said. She did realize that Claire's ball was a huge success, or as the *ton* termed it, a sad crush.

Robbie hovered nearby the entire evening, and claimed his two dances permitted by society's stringent rules. He danced, however, with no other. Claire's glance followed him often, and there was little doubt of their commitment to each other.

Elizabeth danced the last dance, and then quietly went to her room. She was thoroughly bewildered. How could Travis hold her and kiss her, kiss her so warmly, and then leave without a word of explanation? Why had he asked her to forgive him? Her maid Susan was waiting for her, having laid out her night rail and robe.

"Susan, you should not have waited up for me! I am perfectly capable of undressing myself, and it's so very late!"

Susan looked scandalized at the thought of not being available if she were needed.

"La, Miss, you look that tired. Of course I'm here to help you. Let me brush your hair for you, that always makes you feel better. All that lovely hair must be a weight to carry around, though I'll wager half the ladies at the ball would die to have it. Did you have a wonderful time, milady?"

Elizabeth rallied enough to give her a tired smile.

"It was an exceptional ball, and Miss Claire looked as beautiful as an angel. She was a great success."

"You looked just as beautiful, ma'am. Sure and there were never two young ladies as lovely as you two. Did you dance every dance?"

Easing Elizabeth out of her gown, Susan gently unbraided her mistress's hair, and brushed the heavy coils into a shining mass that fell to her hips. Fatigued to the bone, Elizabeth soon found herself in bed, and yawned convincingly enough to make Susan scurry through her duties and leave.

She lay awake for a long time, going over and over the scene in the library. Why had he kissed her so deliciously and then walked away? Did she mean anything to Travis, anything at all? Surely she meant more to him than a duty he was obligated to protect. Then why had he left her so abruptly? Why had he left the ball?

She alternated between feelings of bliss at his caress and despair at his departure. It was a long time before she fell asleep. Then it was an uneasy sleep that had her waltzing in her dreams with a Travis who sneered at her when she stumbled. One who turned away when she tried to clutch him to her and beg him not to leave.

Chapter Twenty-Six

A WEEK AFTER THE BALL Elizabeth came to a decision. She didn't know yet how to implement it. But she was determined to seduce Travis.

It was quite a deliberate decision. She was a grown woman, and it was her body to do with as she pleased. She knew she would be changed, that persuading Travis to show her more of the joys of love would mark her thoughts and the rest of her life. She was not being impulsive; she was simply determined.

Through the last days, she'd felt him deliberately rejecting her. His courtesy and kindness never faltered, but he was obviously striving to put a distance between them. She caught him looking at her more than once, with a sadness in his gaze she didn't understand. He was cured, wasn't he? If he could waltz so gracefully, certainly he was cured. Shouldn't he be happy and confident? And if he was cured, and cared for her, what was keeping him from declaring himself?

The same gaze sometimes seemed to smolder, hinting of his physical desire for her, yet he made no move to be with her. She did not understand him at all, and was apprehensive his plans for his future did not include her. One obvious answer was that he did not truly care for her. While that thought devastated her, it didn't affect her decision. Even if he didn't care, even if he disappeared and she never saw him again, she still wanted the lessons that he alone could teach. He was her only chance at knowing more of physical love, since she would never accept another man.

She waited until the whole house was asleep. She put on the thinnest and most transparent night rail she owned, the demure bow at the neck mocking the glimpses of her erect breasts. Her already pointed nipples and the dark golden thatch between her legs were clearly visible. She swallowed once, and stole quietly to his room.

He must have been awake, for he immediately answered her light knock, tying the belt of his black velvet robe, his hair tousled. His legs were bare, and she suspected he had nothing on under the robe. All the better, she thought.

She saw a glowing spark, deep in his eyes, as he opened the door and took in her attire.

"Elizabeth." It was the barest breath.

"Since you will not come to me, Travis, I have come to you." Her voice did not quaver, and her chin was held high.

Travis did not betray his appreciation of her appearance, nor of her bravery. He straightened his body that seemed to be leaning to her of its own accord. *Dear God*, was his only thought, *may I have the strength to turn her away!*

He opened the door and motioned her in, then closed the door. It would not do to talk in the hall.

"You should not have come, Elizabeth. I don't like to send you away, but I must."

"Then why did you let me in?"

She could not keep the note of despair from her voice. She had not expected him to be so blunt and so adamant. She'd thought she might have to persuade him, hoping he wouldn't make it too difficult. She had not considered what she would do if she failed.

"Elizabeth, I have no wish to go into this. It will benefit neither of us. Please leave before you say what I do not want to hear."

Something in Elizabeth snapped.

"Why are you turning me away? Don't you want my body? After all, you have already had it, why not have it again?"

She put her fingers over her trembling mouth as she realized what she had said.

"So," Travis spoke slowly. "I did take you. I thought I had."

She rushed in to reassure him. "It was not your fault, Travis, I urged you on. Truly you must not blame yourself. Indeed, you were not yourself!"

"Drunk or not, and no matter what you say, there is no excuse for me," he said in a bitter tone. "You are in my protection. I should be horsewhipped."

She rushed to him in regret for her words, and his arms automatically went around her. He kept his face turned from her, but she rained kisses on as much of it as she could reach, and with a groan he clasped her to him tightly. He buried his face in her hair for a moment, and then stepped back. Determined to send her away, his lips compressed as he tried to find the words.

"I will not do this, Elizabeth. We are very lucky you didn't get with child last time. I will not take that chance with you again."

She felt his body tense and withdraw, and did not hear his words. The only thing clear was that he didn't want her. No matter that she was throwing herself at him, he did not want her. Why didn't she appeal to him? What was wrong with her that the man she loved would not even take the gift she was proffering with her whole heart? Breaking into sobs, her body shaking with their force, she started to turn and leave.

"It's as I thought. It was only because of the brandy. You would never have touched me otherwise. You would have taken any woman. I don't appeal to you at all."

Travis stared at her in astonishment. He was trying to protect the little idiot! Suddenly she slid to the floor, hiding her face in her hands as the sobs robbed her of strength to move. The sight of her flood of tears shattered his resolve. He could not endure the sight of his proud girl, humiliated in a manner he'd never planned or wanted. How could he let her feel she was anything but desirable? Yet how could he encourage her in an act that could ruin her?

Going to her, he sank beside her and gathered her into his arms.

"Elizabeth, listen to me. You are the most desirable woman I have ever known. I have been hard put to keep my hands off you. Day after day I have fought my desire. Surely you know that?"

She merely shook her head and tried to shove him away. He clasped her more firmly, pushing her flat on the floor so she could not move, and lay down beside her. He threw one leg over her body to hold her motionless and opened his mouth on her lips. As soon as he kissed her, she stopped shaking her head and quieted. Dear heaven, he hadn't meant to kiss her, but now it seemed he couldn't stop. She soon began returning his kisses, letting his velvet tongue inside to pleasure them both.

Travis groaned.

"How can you think I don't want you? A man cannot pretend he wants a woman. You must know I am more than eager to have you. It is something no man can fake. Can't you feel me, Elizabeth?"

Oh, yes, she could feel him. He was hard and huge, and pressing into her stomach in the way she remembered. She looked up at him solemnly, and what she saw must have reassured her, as she gave the ghost of a smile. Still the tears ran down her cheeks.

Travis was completely undone. If he turned her away, he could scar her for the future. What torment it must be for a sensitive woman to think she was undesirable! If he took her, there would be great pleasure for both of them, but at what cost? He imagined that the last time he had not shown her what loving could be. He must have been a drunken lout. He was trembling from head to toe, as he held Elizabeth closely and prayed he was not talking himself into doing what he wanted more than his next breath. He buried his face in her hair, as his physical state grew more painful.

He took a great gulp of air. There was only one solution. After all, he had already seen to it that she was not a virgin. He would have her again, and show her with his body the love he didn't dare put in words. He'd make certain she knew that she was the most desirable woman who had ever lived. He also vowed he wouldn't leave his seed in her. He slanted his lips over hers, tentatively, then deeply, and was lost.

Travis broke away and got to his knees.

"Please," Elizabeth breathed. "Don't stop now."

Travis looked at her, the fire in his eyes blazing.

"I won't stop. Nothing could stop me now."

He scooped her up in his arms and arose. "I don't intend to school you in pleasure on a hard floor, when there is a perfectly good bed handy."

Covering her face with little nipping kisses, he carried her to the bed and laid her on it. He leaned over her, his hands reaching for the bow at her neck. In a daze of passion, Elizabeth suddenly realized he had somehow stripped her gown from her. He stood looking down at her, while his eyes burned even brighter.

"You are exquisite, Elizabeth. Any man in the world would want you. You are every man's dream."

He quickly shrugged off his robe and followed her down, but not before Elizabeth had glimpsed the size and strength of his arousal. She had not really seen him the last time. He covered her gasp with his lips, murmuring to her as he began to caress her body in a way she'd never imagined. She soon forgot what little fear she had, as his clever hands began to weave a magical spell around her senses.

He kissed her with lips that were slightly parted, but he didn't want to rush. She deserved every joy he could give her, and he meant her to have them. He'd probably given her little satisfaction before. This time would be different. Part of making her know her desirability would be worshipping her with his hands and his body.

And so he leaned over her, letting his hands freely roam and touch every delectable surface. He wanted her warm and writhing before he moved fully over her.

He circled her erect nipples with his thumbs, bringing more small gasps from her. He followed his thumbs with his lips, kissing and pulling while she bucked with pleasure. He put one hand between her legs and felt her warm moisture, and knew she was ready for him, but still he did not hurry. He found the heart of her desire unerringly, and began to caress it, watching her dazed face closely. She began to twist and pant, not knowing what she wanted.

And Travis rejoiced.

Finally, fully aroused, he put his sex at her entrance, and slowly pushed into her. Her sudden intake of breath made him suspect he'd not been this large when he had taken her before. Small wonder, he thought. He'd not only been foxed, he'd probably selfishly rushed matters. While he might come to regret what he was doing, at least he was going to do it well!

His jaw set, Travis rigidly held himself back to make sure she'd expanded to take him in. Then he began to move, slowly at first, then faster, but always in command. He waited until he felt her muscles start to contract, and then reached down with his hand between their bodies and brought her fully to climax, smothering her cries in his mouth.

Controlling himself was even harder than Travis had expected, but he stayed in her as long as possible, until he was sure she was experiencing the pleasure he wanted her to have. At the last moment, he withdrew and spent his seed outside her body. It was not the ultimate fulfillment he would have liked, but it was all he'd allow himself, and indeed, since it was Elizabeth, he was well satisfied. More important, he knew that she had found pleasure and she wouldn't have a child from his self-indulgence.

ELIZABETH WAS A MASS of sensation, her body consumed by the fire roaring through her. She dimly realized he'd shown her a pleasure she'd not known existed, and shuddered with the force of her feelings.

She fell into a slight doze, and came out of it only when she felt Travis cleansing her stomach and between her legs with a soft, warm cloth. She sat upright, more shocked at his performing such an intimate service than she'd been at their joining.

"My lord, you cannot do that," she stammered.

Travis chuckled, a deep throaty chuckle that showed the depth of his surprising amusement.

"What a moment to go back to calling me milord! Surely this is not the time or the place."

She reddened and laughed with him.

"It does seem ridiculous. But you are acting as my servant, and that seems wrong."

His face grew serious, and taking the basin of water and towels to a small table, he returned to her side and looked down at her.

"Elizabeth, if you only knew how pleased I am to be able to do any service for you, you would not quibble. You've given me remarkable pleasure, and I am deeply grateful. I will never forget what I owe you."

She flushed again, thinking that she was the one who was grateful. She'd never dreamed such bliss existed. Something nagged at the edges of her dazed mind, that the experience had somehow not been the same for him as the last time. But he seemed at ease, and was looking at her with a loving affection in his eyes.

He took her shoulders gently and pulled her up to a sitting position.

"I would like nothing better than to have you spend the night in my bed. Since that cannot be, I must see you safely to your room. Do you think if you wrapped this blanket around you, you might stay warm till you reached your own bed? I'll make sure the hall is clear."

She was being dismissed. However kind his words were, he was telling her she must leave. She did not in the slightest care if her reputation were ruined. She didn't want to leave him.

With a sigh, she realized he was giving her no alternative. Tucking a blanket around her, his hands lingered and lightly caressed her shoulders. Then he opened the door, looked out, took her hand, walking her down the hall to her own room.

He opened the door and took her briefly in his arms, dropping his cheek to the top of her shining head, and standing silently.

"Thank you so much, my very dear. Be safe," he whispered to her and was gone.

She climbed into bed, still in a haze of contentment. His parting words seemed somewhat strange to her, however. Were they the words of a lover, or not? She tumbled into sleep, not sure of anything except that she would never, *ever*, regret going to Travis' room.

Chapter Twenty-Seven

ELIZABETH SAW LITTLE of Travis in the next two weeks. He closeted himself with his man of business and his lawyer for much of the time. The rest he spent walking. He didn't need the cane anymore, but took it with him, swinging it as he strode down the street. He was gone for such long stretches Elizabeth thought he must have covered half of London. Certainly he was not accessible to any of his family, and Elizabeth soon became sure his isolation was deliberate.

Once again she alternated between euphoria and despair. She didn't believe their joining had left him unaffected. It had changed her life. She'd known rapture in his arms, and felt completely vindicated in her decision to go to him. Even if she never knew such joy again, she would always remember every moment, and the memory would guide her the rest of her life. If the lonely, long nights she feared were to be her future, at least she'd have joyful memories.

There could be no man for her but Travis. She'd known that for some time, but not with this certainty. And so she watched and waited. Surely when he worked through whatever problem bothered him, he would turn to her.

Her certainty faltered when she went one morning to breakfast, and found Lady Rivington, a note in her hand, and her face troubled. She spoke to Elizabeth.

"I do not know what to make of this. Perhaps it will make sense to you."

She handed Elizabeth a single sheet of paper, and Elizabeth immediately recognized the distinctively heavy scrawl of Travis.

'My dearest mother,' she read, *'By the time you receive this I will have already left. Please do not worry about me. Phillips and I will be gone for an indefinite time. You will not be able to reach me, but my man of affairs had explicit instructions. Either you, Claire, or Elizabeth can go to him at any times for*

*whatever matter needs attention. You have only to send for him, as I believe he
knows how to deal with any eventuality.*

*I hope you will forgive me if this causes you any concern. Rest assured it is for
the best, and something I sincerely want. I will be in touch as soon as I can.*

With my love and respect to you all,

Travis.'

Her eyes filled with tears, Elizabeth sat with her head bowed. She was
even more bewildered than before. Where could he have gone, but more
importantly, why had he left?

Lady Rivington patted her hand, and spoke gently.

"I see I don't have to ask if you have any knowledge of this. You are
obviously as stunned as I."

Elizabeth lifted her dismayed eyes, and handed back the letter.

"But where could he have gone? Do you think perhaps to Cade Manor?"

"If that be so, why wouldn't he tell us? It's true the estate is vast, and could
probably use some personal attention. I'll send a footman at once to check, but
I doubt that is his destination. Why would Travis be secretive about a legitimate
reason such as seeing to the estate? No, that is not his destination."

"And his other properties? I suppose the same reasoning applies to them?"

Elizabeth's bewilderment grew, a hint of panic now entering her disordered
thoughts.

"He would have even less reason to conceal going to one of the smaller
estates."

"But why does he give no hint of when he expects to return? Does he truly
have no idea? It is not like him to be thoughtless, so there must be a reason
behind it all."

Elizabeth had a dreadful feeling that she might be the reason, and that he
intended to stay away long enough for her to get over her infatuation. She'd
certainly made her feelings plain to him. Perhaps too plain. Perhaps he wanted
time to solve the problem of his too-loving ward.

"I do not know what to say, ma'am, except I think it exceedingly unlike him.
I can understand none of it."

She helped herself to coffee, which she drank in silence. Since food did not
appeal to her, she excused herself and wandered to her room.

Lady Rivington looked after her. She'd come to love Elizabeth dearly, and had long hoped Travis did too. At times she'd caught him looking hungrily at the girl, yet he'd never discussed his feelings with her. But then, it had been a long time since he'd come to her with a problem. He was a loving son, but a most self-contained one. With a sigh, she put the letter down. She would show it to Claire and see if it made any sense to her daughter.

"At least," she mused, *"he has taken Phillips with him."*

It was not much of a consolation.

THE DAYS DRAGGED FOR Elizabeth. Claire, with her newfound love for Robbie, was lost in her own world of day-dreaming. While she was concerned about her brother, his absence didn't worry her. After all, he'd survived a horrible war, so she saw little reason to be overly anxious now. They would all know in time where he was and what he was doing.

Elizabeth, who wanted only to think about Travis, found the conversations around her stultifying. She sat listening one day as Missy and Amelia teased Claire about Robbie's absence. Robbie had returned to Stramshire the day after the ball, as he had only come to fulfill his promise to Claire that he would attend. As he had feared, the curate who'd helped out during his mother's illness had been slipshod, especially about the New School.

Amelia sat holding her lovely hands in front of her.

"Can you imagine I would settle for less than as many servants as I want? Can you imagine me using these hands to help out in a country parish? Can you really see me attempting to teach some peasant's child? Really, Claire, I think your wits have gone begging to even consider such a thing! And how can your family countenance it?"

Before Claire could answer, Missy jumped to her defense.

"Amelia, I very much admire Claire for contemplating such things. I don't know if she'll actually do them, but her intentions are to be applauded."

Amelia did not even try to suppress her expressive shudder. Claire meantime, looking even more dreamy than usual, was unperturbed.

"Don't fret, Missy. The future will bring what it will. Amelia has a different goal than I, as we all know, and who knows who is right? Certainly we are each convinced we have the answer. The main thing is my brother and I exchanged promises. I pledged to finish this season, and he promised I could then help choose my husband."

"You're fortunate there." Missy sighed. "Our parents would not give permission for either of us to marry without a title. If Lord Willoughby comes up to scratch, he will be accepted."

"La, Missy," said Amelia, "I think you are all about in your head to envy Claire. There is nothing to envy in favoring the wrong man. Our parents are wise and will do the proper thing by us."

Elizabeth was very hard put to keep from delivering Amelia a proper set down. Claire only smiled, and as Elizabeth thought the conversation verging on repellent, excused herself and wandered off to the library. She'd often found solace there. She had but to close her eyes and see Travis, holding her with a look of what she was sure was more than affection.

But she could not keep her attention long on anything, even her favorite books. Travis, what was Travis doing this very moment? Was he in some kind of danger? When would they hear from him? How she wished she had Firebird, and could gallop away from some of her disturbing thoughts. If Travis didn't return soon, she'd go home to Kimberly. She'd rather be by herself to come to terms with his absence. At least she'd have the solace of the familiarity of home, and wouldn't have to endure shielded but still pitying looks.

Chapter Twenty-Eight

THE BRIGHTEST SPOT in the weeks following Travis' departure was Richard's three-day between-terms vacation. The entire household, after such a period of valiantly suppressed despondency, bloomed under the exuberance of the ten-year-old whirlwind of a boy. Always mannerly, Richard was so delighted to be seeing his sister and London, that everyone's spirits were lifted. Lady Rivington and Claire were charmed by his intelligence, his enthusiasm, and his shining good looks. Lady Lavinia was completely *aux anges*. Elizabeth, determined that he would see no sign of her depression, gave herself up to the pleasure of showing him London. Although he'd not been around recently, David Lansdowne reappeared to offer his assistance.

Sightseeing with Richard was exhilarating. His interest was caught by unexpected items, but when Elizabeth considered them, they were ones that would appeal to a boy. A cannon captured from the French fascinated him. It was seated on a Chinese dragon made of cast iron, and was newly arrived in London. Richard wanted a return visit to the Horse Guards Parade to see it. Hours were spent at the Tower of London, with its double attraction of the Royal Zoo and the Tower's bloody history. He was fascinated to see the green where so many subjects, including two queens, had lost their royal heads. By far his favorite, however, was Astley's Amphitheatre, with its trick horseback riding and acrobats. Fortunately David did not mind going twice, and he seemed not only tolerant but charmed by Richard's energy. David would make a wonderful husband and father, Elizabeth thought. At times she regretted knowing she wouldn't be happy in a marriage with anyone but Travis. Better she remain a spinster than marry with a heart forever belonging to another.

Richard and David were soon on very friendly terms. David didn't mind the boy's endless questions, and enjoyed his enthusiastic response to the exciting world he was finding in London.

They were seated one day at Gunther's, and Richard was on his third ice. Elizabeth thought David indulged him too much, but hated to interrupt their growing enjoyment of each other. They'd just paid a second visit to the French cannon. Suddenly Richard's face clouded.

"I just can't understand why Lord Cade has disappeared. No one seems to have any idea where he is. Even the servants are puzzled. I know he saw many cannon like this one, and could tell us lots of interesting stories."

Elizabeth kept smiling, masking the disquiet that assailed her whenever she thought of Travis' abrupt departure.

She reached over and tousled his golden hair.

"Surely you realize a grown man has affairs and business he doesn't discuss with his womenfolk."

Richard looked at her with undisguised rejection of such idiocy.

"Most men don't go off without a word to anyone of where they are going. And I miss him so. He's such a great gun. I would so like to see him, and I am only here one more day."

"We would all like to see him, Richard," David said.

"And we don't even know when he will come back!" Richard mourned.

Again David saved the situation, as Elizabeth had run out of answers.

"None of us knows, Richard. Which means that when Travis does return, he'll have a fascinating story to tell us. In the meantime, we must be saving up stories to tell him. Don't you think we could tease him about Palisades not being able do some tricks of the horses at Astley's?"

Richard looked a little scandalized at the idea of teasing the aristocratic Earl, but he did turn to detailing the wondrous things they had seen at Astley's. Elizabeth sat listening to him, very pleased with the effect school was having on Richard.

Suddenly she thought of the letter about the bully at school.

"How did you deal with the boy who was so troublesome?" she asked.

"Oh, the Earl wrote and gave me advice. He said if I talked to my two best friends and we tried to include Robert in our activities, he might act differently after a while. I thought it worth trying. I didn't expect it to work, but it did."

So Travis had been thoughtful enough to do something to help Richard. She was not surprised. Travis was a gentleman in every sense of the word.

Richard returned to school, and Elizabeth missed him sadly. He'd enabled her for a short while to think of something other than her longing for Travis. She found the days wretchedly flat once again, and began to long for Kimberly, for the freedom to ride Firebird *vent-a-terre* across the fields, to see her beloved countryside again. But mostly she wanted to be alone. She was tired of forcing herself to be cheerful, of hiding her desolation. She waited one day until she found Lady Rivington in the morning room, sipping her usual hot chocolate. Going to her, she knelt by her chair.

"Dear ma'am, you must know how I esteem you. You and Claire have made me feel like one of the family, and I dearly love you both. But I need to go home. I've never been much of the society type, and while I've deeply enjoyed the privilege of helping to launch Claire, I feel you no longer need me. She is a success, and can now take any path she chooses. But I need my meadows, and my horses to ride. I need leisure to read and to think."

She half-laughed as she added, "I guess the *ton* would call it a 'repairing lease'. All I know is my spirits are sadly out of curl."

Lady Rivington looked down at the girl she'd come to love as a daughter, and stroked her hair. She wished she had some word of encouragement. She'd always adored Travis, but this unexplained absence was testing even her approval.

"My dear, if that is what you want, of course that's what you must do. I don't know how I will go on without you, however. Can you tell me this is only temporary, and that you'll come back to us?"

Elizabeth swallowed the lump in her throat, and didn't answer directly. She did not truly think she'd be returning, but oh, how she wished she could.

"The main argument against my leaving is I will have to take Aunt Lavinia, and I know you and she have become bosom bows. Even in as small a village as Stramshire, I cannot live alone and not be branded a wicked woman. But I promise you I'll look for another companion and send Aunt Lavinia back to you as soon as may be."

"Ever considerate," Lady Rivington murmured. "Dear child, having your spirits restored is more important to me than my personal concerns. Of course I'll miss Lavinia, almost as much I'll miss you. Have you told her yet?"

"Oh no, ma'am, I wanted to make sure you were in agreement. I think she will regret leaving, but will be loyal to me."

Lady Rivington wished she had Travis standing directly in front of her. She would give him a lecture he'd not soon forget. She tried not to worry too much about him, since he had Phillips with him. But as the days went by, and there was no word from him at all, she wondered what possessed him. Where could he have gone? Surely she was not mistaken that he valued Elizabeth, in fact loved her! Why then was he staying away? Didn't he guess he was shattering Elizabeth's heart?

She'd been stroking Elizabeth's bent head during the conversation, and to Elizabeth, it was as if she were being given a benediction.

"Have you decided when you will leave, my dear? Can I help you in any way?"

Elizabeth again had to fight the clump of tears in her throat.

"I think we'll leave as soon as we can pack. I detest prolonged farewells, in fact I don't know how I can say good-bye to you and Claire."

"My dear, the sooner you leave, the sooner you'll return. You know how we'll long for that."

Elizabeth kissed Lady Rivington on the cheek, and went to find Lavinia. As she had hoped, Lavinia raised no protest.

"Of course, my love, if you feel returning to Kimberly will give you some peace, we will leave immediately. You can always return to London if you find that's what you prefer. But certainly you should go now and put your mind at rest. Shall we leave tomorrow, then? I can pack very quickly."

Elizabeth smiled in acknowledgement of her aunt's ready acceptance of her wishes. She probably was incapable of doing wrong in Lavinia's eyes. She didn't think it productive to mention she had no intention of ever returning to London. How could she face London if Travis were not there? Or even worse, how could she face it if he were there, but had planned this absence to deliberately underscore the fact he was beyond her reach? She needed her home, and solitude to mend her damaged heart.

Elisabeth put a great deal of thought into her packing. She didn't feel she should take the gorgeous wardrobe she'd acquired since coming to town. Still, it would be insulting to leave it all behind. She finally settled on three of her simplest morning dresses, one for dinners at home, two pairs of slippers and her half boots. She debated a long while and then added the handsome pelisse of blue sateen. It was technically still summer, yet the evenings were beginning to cool. She was not foolish enough to think her pride would keep her warm. She intended to repay Travis for the garments she was taking as soon as she could.

After Lady Rivington became used to the fact that Elizabeth was not returning, she'd ask that the other garments be distributed to Susan and Claire's maid. It was a compromise position, as she was well aware, but the best she could think of.

Lady Rivington was sweet and obliging, although her eyes followed Elizabeth wistfully. She was adamant on one subject, however. She absolutely refused to let Elizabeth and Lavinia travel by stage, and sent for David.

"After all," she informed Elizabeth, "I would have to answer to Travis if I did anything less. I could not face him if anything happened to you. You will simply have to agree to this one thing, my dear."

"I will be glad of an escort, dear ma'am," said Elizabeth.

In truth she was unreasonably glad to be escorted. Perhaps she had been too long in the atmosphere of Cade House, cherished and privileged as a true daughter.

The day of departure was one of late summer's most seductive. It was a day anyone would be happy to be out and abroad. David drove up in his carriage, emblazoned with the Kingsley crest, and leaped out to hand both ladies in. His eyebrows rose at the small amount of luggage. But he said nothing.

He rode his huge horse, Brandy, alongside. He planned to be able to ride back alone, his coachman following with the carriage. He hated being cooped up in the dratted thing. It took a while to leave the smoky chimneys and dirty streets of London behind.

Gradually the roads became less congested. The countryside was in full bloom. The summer rains had been light but steady, and England was a riot of flowering glory that gladdened Elizabeth's heart. Even so, she found herself forced to concentrate and enjoy the beauty. When she was not careful, her thoughts slipped back to Travis.

So she set herself to appreciate the passing scenery; fields of daisies, the cottages with thatched roofs, sometimes the single spire of a church. The hedgerows were riotous with honeysuckle and geraniums. Once when they passed through a forest, the scent of pine needles seemed to soothe her humiliated spirit. She sat staring out at the beautiful countryside, enjoying it even as she wondered yet again where Travis was, and why he'd left. Surely it was the right decision to go home to Kimberly.

The truth she must learn to live with was that Travis did not want her.

David often rode close to the carriage, pointing out some item of interest he didn't want her to miss. He had amusing tales to tell of previous trips to and from London, and kept the talk light and entertaining. Very thankful for the well-sprung carriage, and its luxurious red velvet squabs, Elizabeth admitted Lady Rivington had been right. Still, when they turned into the wrought iron gates that led to Kimberly, she wished she didn't have to be a good hostess. She would have liked nothing more than to retire to her room and shut the door on the world.

There was, however, the staff to greet and introduce to David. She hugged Melanie and Jimson unabashedly, to their delight. Jimson pretended embarrassment and tried to hide his smile. Melanie had readied a light supper of vegetables from their garden, plus a mildly sauced chicken, and her own incomparable scones. Elizabeth ate little, but David did more than his share.

After dinner, they all sat for a while in the parlor, at David's insistence and refusal to let the ladies retire.

"I want you to have a brandy with me, ladies, before you leave me. I know you're exhausted, and it's often hard to settle to sleep after such a long trip. Just indulge me this one time. Brandy will soothe us all."

David's sturdy good looks and innate charm had captivated Melanie, and she hovered over him with offers of coffee and more cakes. As he refused her with a smile, Elizabeth realized he was right. The brandy was a calming restorative. She also realized she was a poor hostess, indeed.

"David, my dear friend, I don't believe I have even thanked you for dropping all your concerns and offering us your escort. And a luxurious escort, at that. I vow I've never traveled more comfortably."

She buried the thoughts of her trip to London with Travis by her side, and smiled warmly at this dear man who was giving so much, and asking so little.

"Dear David, what would we have done without you? I hope we can make you as comfortable here, as you've made us. Melanie has put you in the blue room. I sincerely hope you plan a long stay, so I can show you this countryside I love."

David looked at her. He felt certain she needed time alone to think through what she desired. She must know that with any kind of encouragement, he'd be at her side. He didn't mind waiting, but he did not want to take advantage of a heart-weary girl. He bowed over her hand, and kissed it lightly.

"Always the perfect gentlewoman, Elizabeth. But I've come to expect that from you. And while I'm happy to have seen this home you love, I cannot stay. I must go back to London tomorrow."

He couldn't decide if dismay or relief was the most prominent on her mobile features. As usual he cherished her naivety.

"If you give me leave, I'll return in several weeks to see how things go with you. And if you need me for any reason, you have only to send word."

He spoke lightly and with just the right amount of polite regret. Still, Elizabeth was not sure he was leaving for a legitimate reason. No matter, it wouldn't be fair to press him to stay. She didn't want to encourage him in any way, even though he he'd given her little sign of a truly serious interest.

If she had ever doubted her feelings for Travis, the trip from London had made them clear. Her thoughts, instead of turning to the pleasures of home, dwelt almost exclusively on him. She didn't know how she would face the long days and nights without him. But she would not unfairly lean on David, even though it was tempting. It was time for her to face the rest of her life.

Alone.

Chapter Twenty-Nine

DAVID LEFT AFTER A leisurely breakfast. He planned to go slowly to give Brandy time to rest. The coachman and carriage would follow after a day's recuperation.

Elizabeth had carefully hidden her desire to be out on Firebird, but as soon as David left, she dragged her father's cut-off breeches from the back of her closet and set off for the stables.

The whole of the stables gleamed, as did the coats of Firebird and Blue Fire. Every stall seemed tidy and well cared for.

She turned in appreciation to Jack Crawley.

"What a wonderful job you've done here, Mr. Crawley! I have never seen the horses or the stalls looking so well! Lord Cade told me of the fire, but I see no sign of it at all."

She had her face half buried in Firebird's mane, but still her satisfaction was evident.

"Sure, and there wasn't that much damage, Miss. All the tenants pitched in and we had things set right in no time."

Actually, there had been much more damage than he wanted her to suspect. He also didn't tell her that Travis had written him before his disappearance, asking that he particularly look after Miss Drayton's safety, if by chance she returned to Kimberly.

The first week passed as well as could be expected, with Elizabeth riding Firebird and Blue Fire for hours at a time, hurtling across the fields and lanes, and glorying in the feel of being once more in control of herself and her horse. Unused muscles and sinews at first protested, but she'd been a horsewoman for too long to let that deter her. Her body soon adjusted, and reveled in the exercise. She found the whole farm in excellent shape. Crawley had somehow managed to get the fields drained and the tenant's houses repaired. Familiar and grateful faces greeted her everywhere she went.

At first it was pleasurable, and then she slowly realized that she was no longer needed as she'd once been. She was loved, and she was welcomed, but she was not needed.

Despair settled over her. She had no place in Travis' life, and now she had no meaningful place in her own home. Once again she mounted Firebird and roamed the countryside, trying to think her way through to an acceptable future.

If she saw Travis again, it would be a constrained meeting about some terms of her guardianship. He didn't want her as a woman, except perhaps as a woman for the night. If he'd felt anything like the thrill that had engulfed her in his arms, he couldn't have left her without a word. He was now making his feelings perfectly clear to her, and she didn't blame him.

She'd pursued him. She couldn't regret that, as at least she had a few memories to see her through the long, lonesome years. She didn't blame him in any particular. He was experienced enough to know that her feelings ran deep, but since his did not, he'd chosen disappearance. Absence to give her time to come to terms with the fact that he was far above her touch.

He was an Earl, and she had no family of consequence, no dowry, no training for the life a countess should know how to lead. She'd thought their mutual love of learning and dislike of superficial social activities to be a bond. She had to face the fact that while they'd enjoyed an unusual companionship for a time, she was not worthy of being his wife. But more than important than this, he didn't want her.

At least he was attempting to be honest. She couldn't like the method he'd chosen, but he was trying in his own way to deal honorably with her.

It was time for her to find some way out of her depression, and so she went to the vicarage. She'd seen little of Robbie, but he'd called several times when she was out riding.

He was in his study when she asked the housekeeper to announce her, and he immediately came out when he heard her voice.

"My dear Elizabeth, how wonderful of you to call."

Before he could say another word, and to her horror, the tears started running down her cheeks. Without a word he gathered her in his arms, holding her as he would a young child who needs comfort. She tried to gulp down her sobs, but he patted her and told her to cry herself out, he had on an old coat anyway.

If he had sympathized with her, she doubted if she could have stopped, but his attempt at humor produced a watery smile and a little stemming of the stream.

He held her loosely but warmly until she stopped and caught a shaky breath.

"Robbie, you poor dear," she said. "I had no notion I was going to dissolve into a watering pot, or I would never have come. And to think I came with a noble idea in mind."

Robbie decided to let her tell him what she willed. Much as he esteemed Lord Cade, the girl weeping in his arms made him wish he could confront him and tell him that his disappearance diminished him as a gentleman. Whatever Travis' reason, he'd devastated a perfectly wonderful girl, and it was not well done of him.

He handed her his large and clean handkerchief, and smiled at her as she mopped at her tears.

"I'm flattered, my dear girl, that I should be the one you turn to. Please, tell me what I can do to help."

"You are a dear, Robbie, but my original thought was to help you, if I could. I admit it would help me tremendously too, as I badly need to be needed. Will you let me take over the teaching of the girls at your school?"

It was evident from the spontaneous grin on his face that Robbie thought this an excellent idea.

"Elizabeth, that's just the thing! If you help, I think more of the tenants and villagers will release their younger girls to you. I have little hope of including the older ones, as they're needed at home. But if I could just make a start with the young ones! If Miss Drayton herself is the teacher, I think it will change some attitudes. Bless you for thinking of it!"

Elizabeth shook her head.

"I can't take credit for something I'm doing to help myself. Jack Crawley is an excellent steward, and one of the most courteous men alive. He faithfully consults me, but it is evident to the merest dolt that he doesn't need my advice. He has the whole estate running smoothly, and I truly am grateful to him. I know Lord Cade's investment will pay off some day, and that means a great deal. But I *have* to find something worthwhile to occupy my days. Or they will cart me straight to Bedlam!"

Her tear-streaked face now had a look of some hope.

Robbie could whole-heartedly thank her and encourage her. His school was still plagued by parents who could see little use for learning, and especially for the girls. Elizabeth would make a difference.

She started the next morning, with two little girls, one of them the Crawley's daughter. By the end of the week another had joined them, and in two weeks she had five. Robbie taught the twelve boys.

She loved teaching. She'd never realized the joy of seeing a young mind take the first steps to unfolding, as their father had tutored Richard at first. Not only did she spend her mornings in the schoolroom, but she enjoyed planning how to enhance the lessons, thinking up learning games, and making out cards that used simple words to teach the alphabet.

School lasted only half a day, so the parents could have the children home for lunch, and also for necessary tasks. Still, she was thrilled at each sign of response or progress, and found she was more cheerful than she'd been for some time.

She often stayed late to straighten up the classroom, and further free Robbie's time. Heavy cleaning was done by the parents, but she usually tidied the room and began her planning for the next day.

She was sitting at her desk one day, working on new words for the spelling cards, when she heard the door open. She did not look up immediately, assuming it was Robbie coming back for something he needed.

A horribly familiar voice greeted her.

"Well, Miss Arrogance, can't you say hello to an old friend?"

She looked up to see Squire Bellamy sneering at her. His eyes were malevolent, his mouth twisted with hatred.

"But, but you have left the country!' she stammered.

"Don't you wish I had, missy! Well, I did, but I came back. I couldn't leave permanently without taking care of you. No one knows where your fine guardian is, I hear. When he returns he'll be sorry he left you, you can be sure of that!"

Elizabeth looked wildly around. Robbie had been gone at least fifteen minutes. No one else would be appearing. She'd never imagined she was in the slightest danger. The school was on the outskirts of the village. She was beloved by every inhabitant. All but this one, whom everyone assumed had fled overseas.

She could see nothing that would help her. The only scissors she had were blunted for the children's use. The slates and chalk were useless. She did have an inkwell. Could she throw the ink in his eyes? She could see how she might blind him in one, but not both.

She saw he had started toward her, evil written plainly on his face.

"Don't worry, Elizabeth, I don't mean to kill you. I might mark you up a bit, you deserve that. But I think first I will enjoy that luscious body you refused to share with me."

He was coming closer all the while he ranted at her.

"I wonder if Travis already sampled your charms. If he has, I won't be easy on you, as your virginity should have been mine. Not that I intend to be easy on you anyway, you understand! You've never known your place."

His hated face was gloating, and he was now directly in front of her desk. She looked at him defiantly, knowing that if he saw her fear it would please him. Still casting around in her mind for how to best defy him, she noticed a stealthy movement by the door, and swiftly lowered her eyes. She did not want him to see hope in them.

"Don't think I'll give in lightly, Squire. I intend to fight you with every ounce of my strength."

She spoke quietly and with dignity. If she could just keep him talking a little longer!

"You bitch, the more you struggle the better I'll like it. Nothing makes a man's tool harder than subduing a reluctant woman. Now get out from behind that desk!"

As he reached for her, she saw a strange man suddenly leap, the heavy coal shuttle in his hand, and aimed at the back of the Squire's head. He connected with one blow, and then kept on striking. The Squire keeled over quietly, probably literally never knowing what had hit him.

The stranger was slight and very ordinary-looking. He immediately took a pair of cuffs from his pocket and put them on the Squire, and then proceeded to strap his belt around his ankles.

"I think that's about it, Miss Drayton. I'll take care of getting him in a safe place. This time he won't escape trial."

At her stunned look, he smiled.

"'Spose I ought to introduce myself, Miss. I'm Evans, the Runner Lord Cade ordered to protect you. I've been nearby ever since milord left, and if you haven't known it, then I did a good job."

Elizabeth started to stand, and then sat back down. Her legs felt as if they were made of rubber. Travis had ordered this man to protect her, even though he deserted her? That meant two things, Travis had not been content with the Squire's disappearance, and he had some feeling for her. Probably just obligation, but still, she felt a flare of joy.

"I'm going for the vicar, miss. You had better come with me. This villain won't be stirring for some time. And when he comes to, he's going to have a fearsome headache!"

Evans evidently thought this was a very funny remark as he cackled all the while he held the door open, and walked her quickly down the street. Elizabeth followed in a daze. She didn't want to be even in the same room with the evil Squire. This competent little man would see to things.

She wanted to go home.

Robbie was not at the vicarage, but his housekeeper gave her tea, fussed over her, and sent a young lad to Kimberly to fetch Miss Drayton's horse. After what seemed to her an interminable time, she reached her home and her room. After persuading Melinda she wanted no more pampering, she sunk limply into the big chair by the window. She was surprised she felt calm, although still shuddering at the thoughts of what would have happened without Evans. Still, Evans had been there. And he'd been sent by Travis. The slight fluttering of buoyancy persisted, even though she told herself it was just Travis' scrupulous safeguarding of those under his care.

Chapter Thirty

FORTUNATELY FOR ELIZABETH, the next day was a Saturday, and she did not have to face the schoolroom where she'd been so nearly assaulted. She thought it would be a while before she could erase the image of Bellamy advancing on her, hatred on his face and rape in his heart. Peculiarly lazy, she decided to work in the herb garden. There was something very satisfying about working the soil and freeing the garden of weeds.

She worked until she was too weary to continue, and then, wandering into the library, picked up a book to read. A light supper with Lavinia was pleasant, but almost silent on Elizabeth's part. But then, she had not felt much like conversing for some time. She took a leisurely bath, and brushed out her long mane of hair. All the little routine tasks seemed to bring her some sort of solace. She dressed in her night rail and old serviceable robe, and curled up in the chair in her bedroom to read.

To her surprise, she managed to lose herself in the pages. Reading was a luxury that she'd not been able to enjoy since Travis left. She wasn't at all sleepy, but for some reason, felt more at peace.

She heard a light knock on her door and expecting Olivia, told her to come in.

The door opened, and Travis stood there. A ridiculously handsome Travis, at least a stone heavier, and bronzed from the sun. He was clad informally, only a frilled shirt and trousers that clung to him and revealed his muscled fitness. Her heart gave a thudding leap in her chest as she stared at him with hungry eyes. Then she jumped from her chair and threw herself at him.

He opened his arms to her, but then, caught by surprise, grabbed her fists as she began to pound on his chest.

"You brute! You, you beast! How could you, how could you?"

Travis felt such a mixture of emotion he was almost speechless. This was his welcome? His Elizabeth, railing at him? Attacking him? And weeping all the while, tears raining down her cheeks?

He held her wrists in one big hand, and soothed her hair with the other.

"You are right, my love. I'm those things and more. But please don't cry, darling. I can stand anything but that."

He bent to kiss her, but she would have none of it, turning away, her brief storm over, the tears continuing to roll.

"I'm sorry," she gulped. "Not for the names I called you, but for weeping. I seem to do that too much lately."

Travis put his arms loosely around her, gentling her with his touch and his lips on her hair. Even though he didn't tighten his hold, he could tell she'd lost weight, and guilt assailed him.

"I am not worth a one of your tears, my dearest love."

Realizing she was letting him hold her, he bent again, and this time, his lips met hers briefly.

"You do not have to do that, you know," Elizabeth said, her voice muffled against his chest. Being in his arms was even more heavenly than she remembered, but she did not want him to placate her like a child. "You do not have to call me your love. I know I'm not. But I will let you come in to talk."

Travis laughed softly. "You are my love. My only love, my dearest love. And I'm already in."

She looked at him with such skepticism and scorn that his heart turned over. Had he hurt her that much? Could he make her believe and trust in him again, or would she forever hold the past few months against him?

He swung her up in his arms and proceeded to the large reading chair and sat down with her on his lap, smoothing back the long hair from her tear-streaked face.

"You are so beautiful. I think it's impossible for any woman to be more beautiful."

This time he kissed her with an intensity and fervor that left her gasping for breath.

She looked at him with all the love she felt plainly visible in her expressive eyes, and with a groan, he kissed her again, this time deepening it and opening his mouth over hers, letting his tongue find the hidden recesses that tasted like honey and Elizabeth. The sheer intimacy of the kiss made her glad she was already seated, as the bones in her legs were melted butter.

He finally ended the kiss, but held her limp body as close to his as possible.

"It seems I must explain myself to you once again. And I'm well aware I must ask your forgiveness. But I left because I loved you. It was the only thing I could see to do."

Elizabeth stiffened.

"Please do not insult my intelligence, my lord. That makes no sense at all."

Travis chuckled. "So we're back to mi-lording me? I'm in deep trouble indeed."

"This is not a joke, Travis. How can you say you left for love? That is beyond absurd. If you had loved me back then, you would have told me and explained why you were leaving."

"I have loved you forever, Elizabeth. I cannot remember a day I did not. But I had to be sure I was completely cured. I didn't want you waiting for me if I were not. I've spent the last few months in the hills of Scotland, walking incessantly, climbing the steepest crags I could find, even jumping from some of them. Phillips and I did quite a bit of wrestling and boxing, and I found out he's disgustingly good at both. If there was a fragment of bullet left, I wanted to know it. I don't think there is. I can finally offer you a future."

Elizabeth reared back in his arms, her face paling with fright.

"Jumping from crags, indeed! You might have easily killed yourself! How could you be so utterly stupid? How could you doubt my love for you? I would have taken you no matter your physical condition! I made my feelings for you embarrassingly clear."

Her blush and the chagrin in her voice alerted him to tread lightly.

"Your possible feeling for me was my guiding hope these last few months. Only my love for you motivated me. You were with me every minute of every day, and my heart soared as the difficult tasks I set myself only made me stronger. I'd not thought myself worthy of any woman, least of all you. I had to come to you whole."

"That was not fair of you, my lord. If you had explained your concerns to me I could have managed much better."

Her tone showed he was not completely forgiven. Maybe he didn't deserve to be.

He bowed his head and gathered his thoughts.

"I think now perhaps it was wrong of me, but at the time I felt it unfair to do otherwise. If I promise to try to be more forthcoming with any future problems, will that help you forgive me?"

He held her back a little so he could look into her eyes.

"My main fear was that you'd turn to another because I had been unable to tell you of my love. I know David has been at your side when I should have been."

The uncertainty in his tone, and the question in his eyes made her reach up and clasp her arms around his neck.

"There has never been anyone in my heart but you, Travis. Never."

This time their kiss was a commitment to each other and to their future. It left them both shaken, but with a joyous feeling of fulfillment.

Anxious to be certain she at last understood him, he whispered to her, "I couldn't come to you as less than a man. You didn't deserve to be tied to a paralyzed hulk. I had to be sure. Will you forgive me, my love?"

She sighed. "It still bothers me a little that you didn't trust my feelings for you. I care for the man you are, not your physical condition."

He stared at her with hunger, his lips beginning to cover her face with little nipping kisses.

"It had nothing to do with trust in you. I needed to prove to myself that I was cured enough to not ruin your life. But I'll try to do better about communicating."

She turned her face up to him. His familiar scent intoxicated her, a scent that was a potent mixture of cleanliness and cologne, and something essentially Travis. His masculine virility was enhanced by the physical toughening he'd taken on, and she could feel his muscles bunching under her hands as she ran them over his chest. His rod pushed into her bottom, throbbing and insistent. He looked at her, a spark blazing deep in his eyes, growing brighter as his gaze raked over her.

"Perhaps I had better return to the guest room," he said huskily. "Melinda let me in and promised not to wake anyone, but if I don't go now it will only get harder to leave you."

"And if I don't want you to leave?"

"I think I'd better, my love. I have a special license in my pocket, and dearly hope we can be married tomorrow, but I'll do the proper thing and wait till the marriage bed to take you again."

Elizabeth looked directly into his eyes.

"And if I do not want to wait? Perhaps I'm not the proper lady for you after all."

Travis looked at her, the flame growing larger and hotter.

"Elizabeth, let me be clear with you. I would love to make this our marriage night. I want to carry you to that bed and not let you out of it for hours. But I've already been most improper with you, and I'm striving to make it right."

Elizabeth reached up and smoothed his hair from his eyes. She held his face in her hands, and spoke as solemnly as he had.

"I have felt married to you since our first night together. A few words tomorrow and a license will not make a difference."

The flame now lit his face, and he deftly held her and rose at the same time. Cuddling her close to his chest, he carried her to the bed and laid her lovingly on it. Returning to the door, he locked it. Stripping off his clothes as he strode to the bed, he was soon naked except for his underdrawers.

Leaning over her, he slipped the robe off her shoulders, and then began caressing her breasts through her thin gown.

"Elizabeth," he groaned, "Are you sure this is what you want?"

"Stop talking, Travis," she sighed against his mouth.

His hands kept moving over her, while his emotions seethed. He literally felt the barriers crash between them. For the first time, he could take her the way she deserved to be pleasured. He could show her his absolute commitment, and he didn't have to hold himself in check. He'd taken her twice before, but under circumstances he wanted to erase from her memory. Tonight was the beginning of the rest of their lives together. He resolved to make it as memorable for her as it would be for him. She was, after all, his one and only love.

He wouldn't hurry. He wouldn't! He wanted to build memories for them both. He lowered himself onto the bed, and reached for her. Holding himself to the side and above her, he lifted her gown and slid her out of it. At the sight of her beautiful body, he exhaled and then lowered his head to taste her breasts.

Taking his time, he lavished his kisses on both of them, and finally settled down to one nipple that he drew into his mouth and sucked greedily.

Elizabeth nearly came off the bed. He smiled, and went back to kissing her all over her body. He wanted to savor her, to make her aware of what possibilities existed for both of them, but most of all to explore every inch of her. Her hair smelled of lavender soap. He knew that no matter how long they both lived, he would never have enough of her.

He moved his toughened but graceful hands over her body, stroking the incredibly soft skin of her stomach, and then moving lower. When he parted her hot flesh, and found the center of her desire, she bucked and grasped him. To his delight, she was already warm and wet. Still, he kept up his caresses, murmuring words of love that she barely heard. She soon writhed and twisted on the bed, but he held her down, kissing her on the sensitive spot between her legs until she began to convulse. Her eyes flew open with surprise as she shuddered in release and he swallowed her cries of passion. Still trembling, she sank back onto the bed, stunned by her climax. Her eyes flew open and he held her tightly until she quieted.

"What is it, love?" he managed to ask.

"It was not like that before," she gasped.

Of course it hadn't been. This time they were truly making love. He was incapable of answering her verbally, but he kissed her deeply and then moved over her.

She'd felt satiated and replete, but as he renewed his caresses, Elizabeth was astonished to find she was again climbing the mountain of delight he provided. With a moan, she tightened her arms around him. When he entered her again, she moved with him, arching her body into his, and wrapping her legs around his waist to draw him deeper. She gave him not only her body, but her whole being.

Keeping pace with him, he increased his thrusts, so that soon they peaked together. Cradling her in his arms, he rolled over to his side, afraid of crushing her. Still joined, he kissed her face and her lips, in adoring gratitude, and in amazement that the act of love could be this magnificent.

Wrapped in his arms, she fell into a light doze, a smile of pure delight on her lips.

She awoke a little later to find him again filling her, the embers of his passion glowing just as brightly as before, and warming her very soul. What a delightful way to be wakened! She gave a little wiggle of enjoyment. Her sweetly spontaneous response made Travis gasp, and forget his resolve to give her a slow, deliberate loving. It was an instantaneous combustion they were powerless to control, a frenzied mating, amazing them both. It was over quickly, and they found themselves clutching each other as their thudding hearts began to slow.

Completely awed by the power she had over him, Travis pulled her to him for a grateful lover's kiss.

"I didn't mean to take you so quickly. But you can make me forget any resolve, no matter how worthy."

He buried his face in her hair, taking tresses of it and winding it around his hand.

"You are everything any man could want, Elizabeth. Will you allow me to marry you today, with Robbie doing the honors, or do you want to wait for a large wedding at St. George's? You'll be a countess, you know, and you can have whatever you desire. If you want a big wedding, I can send word to my mother. I stopped to tell her I intended to make you my bride, and she is overjoyed at the prospect of having you for a daughter. What do you want, my love? An immediate and very small wedding, or a large one later? Or do you want something in between that I haven't had the wits to think of?"

He was holding her tightly and automatically moving his hips against hers in a rhythm that made it difficult for Elizabeth to think of anything but the delightful feel of his naked body against hers.

"I would like to be married tomorrow, or perhaps it's now today. Robbie will be delighted to oblige, and I'll finally feel safe. I don't care to subject your mother to the planning of a large wedding, but we can repeat with a small ceremony in London if she desires. If you feel differently, just say so. I've been yours in my heart for so long that the words don't really matter."

He took her lips in a long, drugging kiss.

"I'd feel better to have it done immediately. We've had too much delay already. I still shudder at how close you came yesterday to utter disaster."

At her look of astonishment, he said, "Of course I've kept as close track of you as I could. Evans filled me in on the details early this evening, and I'll make sure this time Bellamy is deported to Australia and that he never escapes. I want you by my side and in my arms as soon as possible. Besides, I want to claim you before the world as my wife and my countess."

Her love glowed in her eyes, such a shining thing that he felt humbled.

"Then let's go find Robbie as soon as we can."

She chuckled. "I don't imagine Aunt Lavinia is ignorant of your presence in my bedroom. Very little goes on that she doesn't know about, but she'll not censure me. She's long guessed how much I love you, and she'll be nothing but ecstatic that we are marrying. And as for Richard, he'll be in alt!"

He gave a mock sigh.

"To think you're marrying me just to please your relatives!"

In spite of his teasing tone, she answered seriously. "I can't remember when I didn't love you."

The look and the kiss he gave her were as much a pledge as the words they'd soon say to each other. It was a kiss of unconditional love, an acknowledgement that their love had been tested and would weather future trials. In a few hours they would pledge themselves to each other, mind, body, and soul, but the words would only repeat what their hearts had already spoken.

They lay quietly for a moment or two, each of them thinking of the wonderful change their entwined lives would soon undergo, and rejoicing in their love.

She finally stirred.

"I think we'll have to soon arise and face the world. I suppose you must go back to the guest room for what remains of the morning. I hate to let you out of my sight, but I guess I must eject you from my bed, my elusive Earl."

"You will find me at your side from now on," he whispered. "Through all the days and nights and years. I resent each moment that keeps us apart. But I'll leave now, and try to present a respectable appearance when they wake me in the morning."

His hands were still moving over her, lingering at times, and then continuing as if they could not bear to stop.

"Just one more kiss," she murmured, clasping her hands around his neck and drawing his willing lips down to hers.

And before he left for a temporary separation, she smiled and tugged at him, and they once again found their own delight.

At last, their future was here.

About the Author

I'M AN AVID CALIFORNIAN, with a short stint living in upper New York that made me appreciate the wonderful weather here near San Diego. Have two kids, two grandkids, all of them smart and beautiful, of course! I'm lucky to write full-time as that's long been my goal. In fact I'm just plain lucky, and thankfully always have been. Am delighted *My Elusive Earl*, a long historical, is about to be published. I love long historicals with lots of research and interesting quotes. Honest, they're really fun to write and I hope fun to read. Have written erotica, sensual, fanciful, historical and in between. All of them are absorbing in different ways.

Did I mention I loved to write?

Did you enjoy My Elusive Earl?
If so, please help us spread the word about
Jean Hart Stewart and MuseItUp Publishing.
It's as easy as:
•Recommend the book to your family and friends
•Post a review
• Tweet and Facebook about it
Thank you
MuseItUp Publishing

More by Jean Hart Stewart

Spies and Roses
Christmas with the Marquis
Guilty Secrets
Song of the Mage Series
Quest for Magic
Victoria's Visions
Seducing Simon

MuseItUp Publishing
Where Muse authors entertain readers!
https://museituppublishing.com
Follow us on Facebook:
http://www.facebook.com/MuseItUp
and on Twitter:
http://twitter.com/MusePublishing
—for exclusive excerpts of upcoming releases
—contests
—free and specials just for you
—author interviews
—and more!